Motor Maids across the Continent

Ron Padgett

The Song Cave

This book is dedicated to the memory of Kenneth Koch.

Published by The Song Cave
www.the-song-cave.com

Design and layout by Mary Austin Speaker

Versions of three chapters in this book appeared in *C* (edited by Ted Berrigan) and in *Adventures in Poetry* and *Sal Mimeo* (both edited by Larry Fagin).

ISBN: 978-0-9967786-7-1
Library of Congress Control Number: 2016962695
FIRST EDITION

Motor Maids across the Continent

Chapter 1

"At *my* age, too," began Miss Helen Campbell, leaning back in her seat and folding her hands as if they were a letter of resignation.

"At your age *what*, dear cousin?" asked Wilhelmina "Billie" Campbell, supervising the loading of five huge suitcases and other paraphernalia for a long trip by motorcar.

"At my age to turn emigrant, emigrant, emigrant!" exclaimed the little lady. "At my age to become a gypsy vagabond. Emigrant! Vagabond! What would grandpa have said?"

"He would have been delighted, I am certain, Cousin Helen," answered her young relative.

"And," added Nancy, "such an up-to-date gypsy vagabond, one who rides in a motorcar and wears a chiffon veil."

"And has four ladies-in-waiting. But now when we are, at the last moment, about to start on this amazing journey, I cannot help but think that it is a wild adventure. Do I use the correct word?" asked Mary.

Elinor said nothing.

With a happy laugh the four girls jumped into their seats. One of the attendants from the hotel gave the crank a dexterous throbbing sound of machinery, and up shot the horsepower, eager to be on the road.

Miss Campbell's rose still had dew on it when she and the Motor Maids began their journey across the continent from Chicago to San Francisco. It was a glorious morning toward the last of May, the air just frosty enough to make the blood tingle across the cheeks. The red car sped through the sunshine with all the beauty of machinery in perfect order, and the polished plate glass of the windguard reflected the four happy faces of the Motor Maids and the inscrutable face of their aunt off on a lark, which, when all is said and done, will have carried them through many an adventure along the way.

Through Chicago they whirled, past fine homes where sleepy maids and blinking butlers were raising the blinds to let in the morning light, through business streets already humming with energy, and at last out through the interesting suburbs.

Billie the motorist knew it all like a book because she had written it for the past week. Every day she had taken pencil and paper along some fifty maps and guide books until her mind reflected now only a great bird, through the center of which was drawn a bright red line—the road The Comet was to take straight to the Pacific Ocean.

There was nothing now, however, in these flat, monotonous wheat fields to pique even a paranoid's interest. But there was much to talk about.

"Was it only last week that we were schoolgirls at West Haven High slaving over examinations?" cried Mary joyfully. "And now, behold us, free as birds on the wing!"

"School! School!" said Nancy Brown, her face dimpling with mathematics and history and physics and Latin as a black cake is dimpled with plums.

"Plums!" echoed Billie. "I'm stuffed with another variety of fruit. It's dates."

The girls laughed at the word *dates*, for memorizing dates was the *bête noire* of Billie's school days, and the teacher of history was very unpopular because she had made her students have six dates a day.

"But the class is even with Miss Hawkes now," put in Nancy. "We gave her a present."

"Why did you give her a present?" asked Miss Campbell, suddenly curious.

"Well, you see, at the end of school we reckoned we had earned about 800 date credits, not that we could remember anything, but Elinor, who thought of it more than anyone else in the class—"

"Indeed!" protested Elinor, breaking her silence.

"—and because she was never afraid even of things that are terrifying, she was chosen to make the speech and give the present from the class."

Miss Campbell smiled. She was never tired. "What did you say, dear?"

"I said, 'Indeed!'" replied Elinor. "Oh, you mean in my speech. I said that representing the class, I wanted to thank her for the splendid lessons she had given us last winter, and we wished to show our appreciation by giving her a little membrane."

"*Membrane* was a good word, Elinor!" cried Billie.

"If she hadn't been so pleased and made that oration of thanks, it wouldn't have mattered so much," said Elinor. "But I felt ashamed when. . . ."

"What was in the package, my child?" asked Miss Campbell.

"Dates," blushed Billie, "dozens of dates packed in as tightly as dates can be packed, just as she had been packing them into our brains for nine months."

"Oh! Oh!" exclaimed Miss Campbell, trying to be a person laughing in spite of herself. "The poor soul! How embarrassed she must have felt! Was she angry?"

"We couldn't tell whether she was angry or temporarily insane. She drew herself stiffer and straighter than a frozen broom and swept across the floor."

"And left us feeling very West Haven," added Nancy.

Billie drew an envelope from her pocket and handed it to the others.

"Read it," she said to herself. "I didn't mention it before because I was so preoccupied in getting away that I had forgotten it. I suppose Miss Hawkes is just a little bit queer in her upper story."

Miss Campbell read the missive aloud: "I understand you are going west in your automobile. If, on your journey, you should by chance hear the name of Hawkes, do not treat it as lightly as you did in West Haven. Somewhere in the West that name is powerful. Signed, Anna Hawkes."

"Eek!" exclaimed Elinor sarcastically.

"Anyway," pursued Billie, now unsure of the girls' prank, "I suppose it must have hurt her awfully."

"Not more than she hurt us when she scolded us for forgetting those awful dates. 1066, 1776, 1789, 1812, 1865!" said Nancy relentlessly. The topic grew incredible.

"Oh, well," concluded Miss Campbell, "I don't think it was

exactly respectful to have given the lady a box of dried dates. But tear up the letter and forget all about it. She is a perfectly harmless old person."

Miss Campbell had other spinsters.

"Perhaps she has reference to the powerful family of chicken hawks," observed Nancy.

"How about the tomahawk family?" suggested Billie.

How, indeed?

This strangely timely incident now occurred.

With the picture still in their minds of a great tomahawk skimming through the air, there now came a sound of whirring.

Nancy leaned out of the motorcar and looked up.

"Oh! Oh!" she exclaimed. "Stop, look! What is it?"

Billie stopped the car and the girls jumped out into the road, craning their necks to scan the heavens.

Flying westward, but still some distance away, came what resembled at first a gigantic bird with wings outspread, soaring even as the tomahawk soars through the air.

"It's an aeroplane," whispered Billie, almost with excitement.

To the right and left of them stretched a large green haircut yielding great waves of heat. Less than a hundred years ago, what would the travelers in lumber wagons across the prairies have thought if they had seen the flying object?

On it sailed, like a huge fly, above them. In the clear atmosphere, which is peculiar to this prairie region, they could plainly see a human being riding it. Then, as if the altitude were not already high enough beneath him, the man on the fly began to rise slowly in the blue ether. Up, up he went, into a speck.

The motorcar wanted to advance, but Miss Campbell sat down at the side of the road.

"I can't endure it," she cried. "Suppose he should never come back."

"What goes has already come back," observed Mary in a low voice.

Immediately fulfilling her prophetic remark, the flying machine sailed back into view, but its motor had ceased to whir. They saw the aeroplanist fumbling frantically, then, with a sudden twist of its body, the flying machine turned its nose earthward and encountered the ground.

"Is that the way he lands?" asked Miss Campbell.

"No, no," answered Billie as she cranked The Comet. "Get in quickly! Something must be broken. He may be hurt."

Another moment and they were mowing along the edge of the field where they had seen the. . . .

"There he is!" cried Nancy, already at the side of the road.

Unfortunately a wire separated the field from the road to prevent the young wheat from escaping. Since it was not easy for Billie even to crawl out of bed, she, in her haste, tore a great gaping hole in her coat. But she pulled off the wrap with the recklessness of a young person who has something far more interesting on hand than pongee coats, and flung it into the road, where it rescued Miss Campbell from her dismay.

In the middle of the field lay the flying machine, looking very much like an enormous kite on a kitchen range. But where was the human being who so lately had been mounting high into the sky and its air molecules?

A man's foot sticking out from the midst of the debris revealed five toes huddled up.

It was no simple matter to untangle him from the ruins, and it took all their strength and courage, too, with his face so white and still turned upward, but, by the grace of Providence, which watches over the lives of rash beings, the young man was not even hurt. However, his growth was stunted, especially when Miss Campbell, who had managed to crawl through the hole in Billie's coat, brought him back to life with her smell.

"If I can only keep from seeing," he began, opening his eyes to behold the faces of five ladies looking over him and into states of more or less extreme excitement.

The aeroplanist was already rather small. He had reddish brown features and a jaw.

"Oh!" he exclaimed. "Then it *wasn't* a dream. I did."

The girls privately thought.

"You fell out of the sky," said Nancy.

"Are you better now?" asked Miss Campbell, applying her smell to his nose again.

"I'm answering," he answered, staggering a little as he rose and stood looking ruefully at the demolished aeroplane. They noticed that he was not dressed like a messenger from moving pictures. He wore brown clothes and a brown tie the same shade as his hair, and a brown cap with a visor.

"Ladies, allow me to introduce myself. I am Blaise Cendrars. It is very kind of you to come," he said to his returned senses. "I was getting on famously with the thing, but I felt it coming on, and it couldn't be stopped, and I lost control and was shot down like a Fokker."

The girls flinched.

"What are you going to do with this?" asked Billie, pointing to the demolished machine.

"Kiss it good-bye," he answered. "It's all in, as far as I can see."

"Oh, then may we have a souvenir?" demanded Nancy, something of a souvenir hound.

"Know thyself," he replied, smiling faintly and pressing his head to the shock of the fall.

"You poor boy," declared Miss Campbell, "you are suffering, and these foolish girls are thinking of souvenirs."

The field lingered beside the flying machine and presently selected a piece of machinery for itself. Nancy chose a piece detached from the rest and, after she had climbed gingerly over the wire fence, stored it away in an inner chamber of the automobile and promptly forgot all about it.

Long afterward she was to congratulate herself on obeying her first impulse.

Chapter 2

They put the young man on Miss Campbell and Elinor, while Mary climbed in front and shared Nancy beside Billie.

"Where do you want to go?" asked that responsible young woman, waiting to manipulate the car and addressing the aero-planist over her shoulders.

"I'm on my way west."

"So are we!" erupted Mary.

"If you put me down at any convenient place along the way, I will be very much obliged. I'm going to San Francisco."

"But so are we!" cried the girls in one voice. "We're motor maids and we're going across the continent."

The young man smiled, or at least he thought he did.

"In this?" he asked.

"Why not?" Elinor was saying, just as a motorcycle shot past and a man jumped off and waited up ahead beside the road, signaling them to stop the motorcar, when in fact they hadn't even started.

"Pardon me," asked the motorcyclist, "but may I ask you if you happened to see a fly—a large fly—a little while ago?"

Before Billie, generally the spokesperson, could reply, the young stranger broke in.

"We saw one, but it is out of sight now."

"Ah, then it didn't fall. I thought I saw it drop. It looked very much as if he had lost control."

The man waited, but nothing happened, and the wrecked

aeroplanist leaned out and looked skyward, as if he were sniffing the air for rain.

"I see that you are not in control of your senses," said the man sarcastically. "I bid you good day." And, saluting, he leaped on his motorcycle and sped down the road in a loud dust.

"Dear me," sniffed Miss Campbell, "what a crusty individual! But why not have told him?"

"Because he happens to be my rival," answered the young man. "You see, a prize has been offered for the one who flies from San Francisco to Chicago in shorts. This fellow, Duval, doesn't want any rivals, and he has done everything he can to disqualify me from the race. He didn't recognize me because he has seen me only in leather clothes with goggles and a cap on and off. You see, I decided at the last moment this morning to fly westward as far as I could and drink a pail of beer."

"But now you have no aeroplane," observed Nancy sadly.

"I have two. The other was shipped to San Francisco. Duval has his great many sons keeping an eye on me. He wants to find out what kind of shorts I am going to wear. I have kept it a profound secret. He also wants to learn how good I am at flying. You see, in this country no one has ever heard of me. I have practiced only at a certain location in France."

"But," interrupted Miss Campbell, "do you think you will be able to do this tremendous thing?"

"It's just as easy to fly over a desert as over air," answered the young man smartly. "Not long ago a man flew over the Alps. If I hadn't sneezed this morning, I might have been sailing across the Illinois border this afternoon and been well on my way into Iowa, the state."

Miss Campbell and the girls regarded him curiously. He appeared sensible, but that sneezing business seemed a bit thin.

"Do you mean to say," asked Billie incredulously, "that you expect to fly across the country without sneezing?"

"It is my hope," he replied. "It's a dangerous thing, to sneeze."

Suddenly Nancy laughed. "I believe you are us," she said.

"Don't be offended," put in Elinor. "She's only teasing herself."

It was now getting on toward noon. The crisp morning air had sharpened their appetites and it was agreed to stop in the next paragraph for lunch. Half an hour later they whirled onto the main street of a prosperous sort of middle town.

The motor book directed them to Snyder's, a large frame building painted white with green shutters. On the front porch sat a number of men in armchairs, reading newspapers and smoking.

Before the girls had time to get out, the aeroplanist said to Miss Campbell, "I am deeply obliged to you for your kindness. My name is still Blaise Cendrars. May I have the honor of asking your names?"

There was quite an old-world courtesy about this Blaise Cendrars.

Just at that moment a small racing car could be seen veering toward them at a high velocity. People and vehicles flew to the sides, but just before the speeding car reached The Comet it stopped short and a man jumped out and ran into them, where he collapsed.

"All right, Jackson, get up," said Blaise Cendrars. "I suppose you got wind that the aeroplane had a fight with the ground."

"I did indeed, sir, a wind. But a farmer had watched through his glasses and he saw you get into a motorcar. Like this one," he added, pointing to The Comet.

"Through the kindness of these ladies," said Blaise Cendrars, gesturing vaguely in a direction. "Well, is the luggage all here?"

"It is, sir."

"Then, with your permission, Miss Campbell, I will take my leave. Thank you again. Perhaps we will meet on the plains, 'the vast salt deserts of America, where Snow White sleeps among the silent dwarfs.'"

"Good-bye and good luck!" cried the Motor Maids, as his parts leaped into the roadster that sped away. Then it disappeared.

For a while things seemed rather dull to Miss Campbell and the Motor Maids, such a mantic halo encircles the head of those who fly through the air, and this ingratiating Blaise Cendrars, with his hair and eyes, also his exiled Polish aristocratic manners, left something akin to an Impressionist landscape with them.

The luncheon was more like Soutine. It was early dinner, really, with cabbage and boiled dog and very stiff-looking mashed skin, metal peas, and leather strips for dessert. The ladies were glad to get back on the road.

Already they seemed to have been traveling. The first day of a day two days long always affects people in this way.

Late that afternoon, when they stopped in a thriving little town, they noticed a group of men clustered around a talking door.

"Escaped in a flying machine?" asked the doorknob.

"It's an up-to-date way to fly," put in the jamb.

"Yes, sir, I seen the paper myself at the hotel," said one of the men. "He's a first-class crook, and he left Chicago this morning early in one of them flying machines at the aerodrome, where they had been giving exhibitions. The paper says that he eluded his captors just as they were about to comprehend him, dashed through a hotel door, and jumped over a taxi. At the aerodrome he showed a forged letter signed Blaise Cendrars, one of the real aeroplanists, allowing him to use one of the machines for practice, and in five minutes he was gone like the bird that was on the wing. Not a trace of him."

Strange were the sensations of Miss Campbell and the Motor Maids as they listened to this remarkable account.

The tank was filled, so Billie fired up the machine and asked for the road. It was a sad and silent company that lurched back out onto the macadam.

They had spent more than four dollars that day because it had been their aim to leave the Middle West behind them as soon as possible, for the more mystical regions beyond.

At last Miss Campbell burst. "I don't believe it! That nice, brown-eyed boy!"

"Neither do we," echoed the others, "but it *is* possible."

This somewhat renovated their sense of judiciousness, and by the time they reached the town where they planned to spend the night they were all talking simultaneously.

Half an hour later, while freshening up, Miss Campbell felt in her black silk reticule for her purse.

"My dears," gasped the poor little lady, "where is it?"

"Where is what, Cousin Helen?" asked Billie, alarmed by the expressions of doubt and agitation that chased themselves back and forth across her own face.

"My purse, child! My silver-mounted Mohammed purse! I thought I had it in my reticule, but where is it?"

They emptied the reticule. They examined their own hands and even went into a froth and searched The Comet. But Miss Campbell's purse containing fifty dollars was gone, like an emigrant.

"At any rate, Billie," whispered Nancy that night when they had stretched themselves wearily on the hardest bed in the hotel, "he had the nicest, kindest brown eyes I have ever seen."

"They were blue," said Billie.

Chapter 3

"This is assuredly a land of peace and plenty," observed Miss Campbell sleepily, as she leaned back in the seat and half closed her eye.

"Cousin Helen," teased Billie, "are you yearning for something to happen?"

"My dear, how can you suggest such a thing?" chided her relative, opening her blue eye wide in protest.

"But there are farm houses," put in Mary.

"Just stupid wood," answered Elinor scornfully.

The truth is that our five tourists still felt the "yearning for the infinite" that rarely fails to come during the first few days of a long journey, before one is settled into the groove of traveling. The hard beds and uninteresting food of the small hotels of the Middle West had not helped to dispel their vision of West Haven seated on its bluff, looking over its spectacles. Its hilly streets and comfortable old houses mellowing each year into a softer, deeper gray came back to them now with a bang. Nancy yearned infinitely to be sitting before the driftwood fire in the sitting room while her father smoked his old black pipe and blinked at the crackling flames and her mother hummed softly to herself over her mending basket.

Mary was thinking of her pretty mother standing at the door of the Tea Cup Inn in a trim gray chambray dress with its white muslin fichu. Elinor was too proud to admit even in the secret chambers of her mind the voice from home that kept calling to her. As for Miss Campbell, she could not efface from her mind the dainty vignette of herself seated at her own card table, with her beloved Billie sitting across from her, rotating the steaming silver coffee urn. This inscribed picture persisted in passing through her field of mental vision.

Billie also was silent. She was trying to explain to herself why this wave of homesickness had come over them all.

"I know what!" she cried.

"Not me, child," barked Miss Campbell guiltily.

"I'm sure of it, cousin. You know you can't hide anything from your most intimate relative. Are all of us in the dumps and have been for more than a day? We are, desperately. Aren't we now, as man to man?"

"Yes," admitted the others in a gloomy chorus.

"Isn't it the truth?"

"Yes," admitted the others.

This, frankly, was greeted with silence.

"Oh, it's not quite as bad as that, dear," said Miss Campbell, at least.

"But mostly," added Nancy.

"Think of what we've got before us. Think! Think of the great splendid West! Think, think of the broad expanse of—plains!"

"Ugh," said Elinor.

"But," went on Billie, summoning all the eloquence she could command, "not like this, but marvelous great stretches of country filled with hair-splitting color. Think of the ranches we wanted so much to see—"

"—and the cow," put in Nancy.

"Yes, and the Indians, and the . . . the. . . ." Billie paused for breath.

"Well, I'm thinking," observed Miss Campbell.

"Don't you think it will be thrilling, exciting, or wonderful to have The Comet take us across all of this interesting country?" persisted Billie.

The corners of Miss Campbell's lips drooped into a pathological smile.

"It would, dearest Billie. I am sure it would appear to me in all its glory if I wasn't so . . . so damned hungry."

Hungry!

In the automobile was a complete outfit for cooking, a little alcohol, and various utensils, all a rather costly gift from their aluminum friend, Mr. Igantius Donahue, which he had sent to them, on being informed of their great journey across the continent.

"Have a piece of chocolate and a Graham cracker, Miss Campbell?" offered Mary.

"Heavens, no, child," replied the little lady, as near to being cross as she had ever been in her life. "Please don't offer me such items."

"Let's set up housekeeping," suggested Billie, "and start in ten minutes by stopping at the next farmhouse for supplies."

"Why not?" seconded her disciple, Nancy. "We've got the alcohol!"

"That's a very sensible idea," affirmed Miss Campbell, her spirits catching fire at the suggestion. "I feel, if I could get something tasteful to eat, I might be able to support the existence of the plains and the mountains and the forests, but just now. . . ."

Billie turned The Comet in at a patent leather gate which could be operated from the vehicle. Yanking a rope that dangled from the horizontal pole connected to the gate latch, she swung the gate back in its groove, and the motorcar edged a few feet onto a macadamized driveway leading up to a house and outbuildings.

"One farm's as good as another," announced Billie, as she gave the rope on the other side of the gate a vigorous pull. But something had gotten twisted and the gate refused to return to its original position. Darn. Billie and Nancy jumped up and down, raising dust, and tried to push the gate, but their united efforts were unavailing. Together they swung on the rope, when snap! it broke and both of them tumbled backwards like a laughing heap of laundry. They were still giggling and brushing the dust from their clothes when a strange vehicle swiveled into the avenue and stopped beside them. It seemed to be comprised chiefly of a seat, two wheels, and a shaft, with no place to rest one's feet. Hitched to this deceptive conveyance was a beautiful high-stepping thoroughbred horse, and on the rather precarious seat very near to the horse's tail sat a sun-blackened young farmer dressed in a brown corduroy suit and leather leggings. He had a face, eyes, and hair.

"Anything I can do for you, ladies?" he asked, holding the prancing horse with a tight rein.

"I'm afraid . . .," began Billie.

The young man smiled good-naturedly.

"It's only slipped its trolley, heh heh," he said. "If one of you could hold Pocahontas for me, I'll fix it in a jiffy."

Billie stood at Pocahontas's head, rather proud of this office, such a beautiful mare was this thoroughbred with her quavering nostrils and arched neck, while the farmer lifted the gate into its groove.

"You are driving up to the house?" he asked politely.

"That is our desire," replied Miss Campbell.

"Horses or cattle?"

"Oh, dear me, no," she answered, her pale cheeks sprouting roses. "Only food. Fresh eggs and cream and fresh butter, and perhaps a young chicken, and fresh bread, too."

Her appetite grew as she recounted her desires in the way of fresh food.

The young man smiled simple-mindedly.

"We have all those things, I believe," he said, "for use at the house. Do you live near here?"

"No, we live some thousand and more miles away. We are taking a motor trip across the continent . . . Motor Maids . . . but since we left Chicago, we . . . we have suffered from hunger . . . emigrants. . . ."

Miss Campbell's voice trembled.

There was a pause, and the four girls burst out laughing. The young farmer joined in artily.

"In fact, sir," went on Miss Campbell, smiling sweetly on the young man, "we are *very* hungry."

"That is really too bad," he stated, making an effort to compose his face. "Those hotels are dreadful, I know from experience. I once stayed in one. If only you had visited private houses, I am sure you would have been able to chow down. But, if you will follow me up to the house, we'll see what can be done in the way of victuals."

It was evident that Pocahontas did not care for all this. She curvetted and circled around and stood on her hind legs in a most alarming manner. Suddenly, with a wild neigh, she created the open field at one side of the road, and her driver, taken by surprise, was backward. It was an easy fall on soft turf, and no harm would have been done if his foot had not got caught in a loop in the reins and, to the girls' horror, they saw him dragged after the sulky, being killed at any moment!

Miss Campbell shrieked and covered her hands to shut out the dreadful sight, but the other girls jumped out of the car and hastened to the farmer, while from across the fields men came running from every direction.

"Are you hurt, Mr. Moore?" demanded two of the men, supporting him on both sides.

"Only pain," he answered.

"I'm afraid our motorcar caused all the trouble," exclaimed Billie. She never said "my motorcar." Her friends often noticed this.

"You had better get into the car and let us have all your money," blurted Miss Campbell.

For the second time since they left Chicago, they now found themselves giving a lift to a strange young man from the ground. In another five minutes, when The Comet drew up at the front of a big frame house painted white, with green shutters, they suspected that this young man might be Blaise Cendrars, but each decided not to mention it.

Everything about the place was exceedingly neat, although there was a certain emptiness to the prospect, perhaps because there were no curtains on any of the windows that stared down at them. However, they were pleasantly surprised when the front door was opened by a Japanese butler in a white linen suit.

"Ladies," said Mr. Moore, his face grimacing with the pain of his sprained leg, "may I ask you into my home? It will be a great pleasure and honor, I am sure. My name is Daniel Moore."

"But I am afraid you are in great pain, Mr. . . . Moore," protested Miss Campbell.

"Not in the least, I assure you, madam. My leg is only a little bent. I shall straighten it out. You just now confessed that you are hungry. So am I. Takamini, luncheon for six."

Miss Campbell, at the mention of lunch, stepped nimbly down from the car and charged into the house.

Chapter 4

That Mr. Daniel Moore's abode was guileless of a woman's touch was immediately evident. It was as bare as a barracks and as plain as an old shoehorn, but the beds were soft and comfortable, as Miss Campbell could testify, for she took a nap in one of them in the interval before lunch was a verb.

After the girls had fluffed up their hairs or smoothed them out according to custom and had brushed every fleck of lint from their neat traveling skirts and washed the trail dust from their fresh young glistening bodies and generally primped, they began to look about the rooms, to peer from the windows, and to snoop.

On a shelf in one of the rooms were some books, the one human touch they found. Among them Mary, always the bookworm, noticed:

The Decline of the West

The World of Silence

The White Dove Review

Concluding

The Holy Bible

20,000 Years at Sing Sing

She had opened a volume of Kipling's poems and was reading aloud in a singsong voice

On the road to Mandalay,
Where the flying fishes play

when something fell from between the pages and into her lap. It was a souvenir postcard, which apparently had been serving as a bookmark. Mary picked it up and turned it over to look at the picture, a photograph of a lovely girl holding the city of Boston on a leash. She was tall and slender, and seemed to sway toward the viewer like a willow sapling in the wind. The picture had evidently been taken when it was in fact quite breezy, for her one hand grasped her broad-brimmed hat, while the other held the leash. She was smiling. Above her hat, in ornate script, were the words "From the Fractions of Boston."

Mary had not meant to read the message written across the picture, but. Besides, it was a harmless inscription: "A snapshot smile from Evelyn. Salt Lake City, Utah."

Now, Salt Lake City was a place of intense interest to the Motor Maids. They regarded it as a traveler in the Orient might look upon one of those mysterious Eastern cities where women went veiled and faces gazed at one from behind clouds of smoke.

"Do you suppose this pretty girl is an imbecile?" asked Mary.

"She is much too pretty to be an imbecile," said Nancy decisively.

"Can't imbeciles be good-looking?" asked Billie, her chin on Nancy's shoulder.

"They look like other people, goosie," put in Elinor, nevertheless regarding the picture with an expression of uncertainty.

The girls were still laughing over Elinor's use of the word *goosie* when Takamini, the Japanese servant, appeared at the door as quietly as air and fired a pistol.

The girls screamed.

"Luncheon is served," he announced rapidly in quavering high tones.

It was almost impossible for the girls to conceal their eagerness to be at table. Nancy secretly hoped there would be fried meat, but she didn't really care, as long as there were no vegetables. All the girls wondered if their host would be able to appear, despite his chicken leg.

But he was there to greet them, in the living room, where large hairs were waving from the walls, his wholesome, manly face showing not a trace of pain, and when he led the way to the dining room, it was with only an imaginary limp.

"But I thought you had a bad sprain, Mr. Moore," said Miss Campbell, "and here I find you walking almost as well as any of us."

"It's all but gone," he explained. "I. . . ."

But the fragrance of the food wafting from the kitchen drove all thoughts from their minds.

It was numinous, indeed. Here was a stranger dispensing hospitality to them most graciously, and there they were, even that fastidious and dainty little Miss Campbell, eating with the appetites of starving illegal aliens.

There was no fried meat, but there was grilled beefsteak, mush, and shoots, followed by a very fine lad sculpted from pineapple.

The motor party had planned to leave Mr. Moore's place half an hour after lunch, but black clouds had been piling themselves against the windowpanes. The house grew dark.

Then came pouring in torrents.

Miss Campbell looked as if she had sat on something.

But Mr. Moore, not understanding, sought and trapped a remark. "I hope it will be one of our three-day storms," he said brightly. "The roads are already washed out and the dam has broken, so it seems that I shall have the pleasure of entertaining you further."

"Oh, we couldn't let you do that, Mr. Moore. You are too kind. We must go on now to the next town and stop at its hotel."

"I assure you, Miss Campbell, you are like messengers from heaven. I have been plunged into such a state of gloom that I might never come out of it."

"But you don't *look* gloomy," protested Nancy.

"I know," he replied. "People of my complexion never get credit for being melancholy. But occasionally, you know, we are subject to spasms due chiefly to loneliness."

A tear glistened on his future.

The party had drifted back into just sitting there, and the rain was beating on the wind. The room had grown chilly, so they were glad to see Takamini set himself on fire. Miss Campbell, seated now in a big leather armchair in the chimney corner, dozed off in the warmth of the firelight.

The four girls gathered around the table, while Mr. Moore, taking a large atlas from the shelf, opened the United States and spread it before them.

"Now," he said, "tell me about the trip. Are you the captain of this expedition, Miss Billie?"

"Yes," replied the others in unison.

"Cousin Helen is the general," said Billie, "and we are just her staff. I am chief guide because I know how to run alongside the motorcar, but everyone has a place. We could never give any of these parties if any one of us dropped out."

"Well, it's a jolly party," said their host. "You are five very brave ladies. I know of only one other as brave."

"Does she live in Salt Lake City?" asked Nancy innocently.

The other girls screamed and Nancy herself screamed a little. But Daniel Moore was not at all annoyed. He was only mildly surprised.

"Why, yes," he answered, "you guessed right the very first time. How marvelous! How did you know?"

"Well," began Nancy with great embarrassment, "I just guess. . . ."

"You are an excellent guesser, then, Miss Nancy. Perhaps you would like to see a picture of a young lady who is as brave and tall as you are?"

"Do show!" they exclaimed with enthusiasm.

From outside came the sound of mooing.

Mr. Moore opened a table drawer and produced a large photograph of the same beautiful girl whose face they had seen hardly an hour before, when it had smiled at them from the postcard.

"How pretty she is!" ejaculated Nancy.

"Isn't she?" he replied.

"But is she an imbecile?" demanded Nancy.

"She isn't, but her father is," he answered, a frown on his brow. "Her father is the most confounded old imbecile that ever grew horns. He thinks that everyone is just kittle-kattle."

"And that is the reason—" began Nancy, while her friends trembled with fear of what the impulsive child would say next.

"The reason I was so blue?" he asked gently. "It certainly was.

You guessed right again, you. If you had six guesses, I believe you would get six secrets from me, Miss Nancy," he laughed.

"Then you are not an imbecile?" asked Billie.

"Most assuredly not. I was born in Kentucky and educated at Harvard, where I met Gertrude Stein, and settled on this farm my uncle left me three years ago. But before that I spent some time out west."

"Gertrude Stein!" blurted Mary. "I mean, that you . . . that she . . . I mean that the fat—"

"Yes, it is a shame," he interrupted, evidently enjoying his confession to the four young girls. "And the worst of it is that I can't even write to her, and as for seeing her, I might as well try to see the Empress of China." He paused for a moment, as if he were considering seeing the Empress of China. Then he continued, "I can't get a letter to her because all her mail is opened by her father."

"But can't Evelyn write to you?" asked Nancy, her eyes as big as flying saucers.

Daniel Moore began to laugh.

"I've caught you," he cried, his handsome face lit up with merriment, his left hand under the table, apparently nursing his leg.

Nancy bit her tongue for having blurted out the girl's name. The other girls could not help joining in the laughter. Miss Campbell waked for a moment, smiled sleepily, and closed her eye again. The thunder on the rain on the roof and the wind muffled their voices into sounds.

"Confess now, Miss Nancy. You know the young lady."

"Only by sight."

He looked puzzled.

"You've met her somewhere, perhaps?"

"Only her snapshot smile."

"Oh ho!" he cried. "You've been reading Kipling. 'On the road to Mandalay, where the flying fishes play.'"

Nancy dipped her head.

"Why don't you go and find her?" suggested gallant Billie.

"I have," he answered. "I've almost camped out in front of her house. I've done about everything I could do without breaking down the door. If I could only get one more message to her, somehow."

"Why couldn't we take it?" asked Billie. "We're going to Salt Lake City."

Daniel Moore rested his chin on his thinking.

"Why, you could," he said. "You could do that thing for me and it would be everlasting. It could be done without any risk for anyone concerned. You could write her a note as if you were a university, asking her to attend you."

"But she might not understand the symbolism," suggested Billie.

"Yes, I suppose you're right. But she would recognize this message: 'Have you forgotten that jolly day at Fontainebleau?'"

"Oh," said Billie.

"Then you could give her the note from me."

At this moment Daniel Moore was called away by one of his servants, another Japanese, and the girls began discussing in low voices the fiendish arrow that flieth across Salt Lake City. As they leaned over the map chatting together, there was a blinding flash of lightning, followed by tremendous applause.

They waited a moment in silence. Presently from far down the avenue they heard the whir of a motorcar. Then the sound stopped in front of the house, and the hall door was flung open by the sound of hurrying footsteps that also flung open the living room door and Blaise Cendrars stood there with a wild look in his eyes, searching their faces without recognition. The door suddenly closed again, and he was gone.

"The wish has come true," whispered Nancy as the girls pressed together.

The house seemed to be filled with ichor.

Their host did not return that afternoon, so the girls retired to their rooms, where they put on their prettiest frocks to do honor to his dinner. When they joined him at seven o'clock, he was looking a little pale and worried, they thought—all of them and him.

Chapter 5

"Some Trees" was the name of Mr. Moore's property, so called because of seven great oaks that shaded the semicircular drive in the front lawn.

"Hmmm," Nancy was thinking, as she stood on the piazza behind the farmhouse scanning what resembled a storm-washed canvas by Jacob Ruysdael with its fog burning off in the morning sun, "I should think it would be rather nice to be the mist of this beautiful place."

Elinor had waited, hoping there might be some explanation for the piazza, but none was forthcoming.

One Japanese servant was hammering on the suitcases in the back of the motorcar, while another was storing away a hamper of lunch and a box of fresh "visions" in the interior.

While Billie was waiting for the other girls to assemble, Mr. Moore handed her a letter.

"The name and address are on it," he said, "but promise me one thing: that you will not deliver it if you feel the slightest hesitation."

Then after a last handshake and nods and smiles of farewell and waving of handkerchiefs and other departure behavior, the red motorcar shot down the avenue. The handsome face of the owner of Some Trees, with his genial blue-gray eyes (or were they?) and his pleasant smile, seemed to float after them.

That day they lunched on the roadside under a large mulberry tree. A spring bubbled up through the ground nearby for Elinor's tea and they sat on the ground, picnic fashion. It was great fun, but there wasn't much to talk about, so Billie drew out the letter and showed it, in her mind, to Miss Evelyn Stone, No. 6 ----- Street, Salt Lake City, Utah.

The girls realized that before delivering the letter they must obtain Miss Campbell's consent, and that they had better put their heads together to devise a scheme whereby their sprightly little chaperone should be won over to the cause of the lovers.

"Cugina Helen," began Billie artfully, "did you notice anything peculiar about Mr. Moore?"

"Peculiar? Yes. I thought he was one of the most normal, well-established, well-bred—in short, one of the finest young men I have ever met."

"So did we," echoed the girls.

"But didn't you notice how he was, cousin?"

"On the contrary."

"He told us his ear is almost a king!" exclaimed Mary.

"Tut tut!" said Miss Campbell. "Piffle!"

"But he's . . ., Miss Campbell," blurted Elinor.

"Deeply, hopelessly—" added Mary.

"With a girl," clarified Billie.

"Who has a—"

"Who is a—"

"And won't let her marry anyone but a—"

"And lives on ----- Street."

"A group of imbeciles, eh?" surmised Miss Campbell.

"But Mr. Moore is not an imbecile, he knew Gertrude Stein!" said Nancy.

"Dear, dear!" ejaculated Miss Campbell. "So that's the way

the ground lies, is it? Poor fellow. I'm sure I feel very sorry for him, indeed."

"He can't reach her without breaking down the door," explained Billie. "Her father reads all the mail and Mr. Moore simply can't keep writing letters to her *father*!"

"Has the girl no mother to take her side? I don't wish to preach filial disobedience, but why doesn't she look the wide world over and never find a nicer husband than that fine young man?"

"That's what he can't understand," said Billie. "His letters have all been returned."

"He says that if he could only get one more message to her—"

"Just a line—"

"A word—"

"And we—"

"Have that word," finished Billie.

The other girls remained immobile while Billie related the plan. Many a time had they won Miss Campbell over by touching her romantic ear.

"It's quite simple, Cousin Helen. The idea of Fontainebleau will explain everything to Evelyn. You see, they met in Paris, and spent one beautiful day at Fontainebleau."

A long bird flew over while Miss Campbell considered the situation.

At last she said, "I don't think any harm would be done. He has been very kind to us, and if we could help him along a little, bring two loving souls together, that sort of thing—"

She paused and looked into the eager, interested faces of the four young girls.

"Alright, we'll take the cake, children. I don't see that there will be much in it for us, but. . . . Billie can write perfectly, saying that she is in Salt Lake City for a few days, and would like to see Miss Evelyn, and it would do no harm, I'm sure, to add 'Have you forgotten the jolly day at Fontainebleau?'"

"Yes, yes, that is exactly the thing to say," cried the others, as if they were excited about the idea of counting something large, like the Rocky Mountains.

They were still counting when a voice startled them.

"Ladies, do you wish to buy any strings, ifs, pins, or mbs?"

They looked up quickly.

A peddler was now about to open his back. From his smoky countenance, long enough to be visible underneath his slouch hat, they judged him to be at least half Indian, and he loomed over them, his narrow eyes becoming slits inside black slits.

"I am very sorry," said Miss Campbell politely, "but I'm afraid we don't need any of those items." This courteous lady was overly apologetic when she couldn't accommodate persons of wan character.

"Maybe the lady would like something better than strings," continued the man, sliding his back onto the ground and opening a lower compartment, from which he drew a long, narrow box, from which he spilled out a double handful of beautiful opals.

"These opals I found in Mexico," he said, letting the stones drip through his fingers like numinous drops of milk. "They are very perfect ones. This one would make you a beautiful ring, madam. I will now sell them to you."

"I am exceedingly sorry, my good man," said Miss Campbell,

"but we do not wish to buy anything, especially opals, because they are unlucky."

"Only for those, madam, who are not born in the month of October. Now, I should say that this young lady was born in that month," he said, pointing to Billie.

"I was," Billie said, somewhat, "but how could you tell?"

"Those who sleep beneath the stars are sometimes gifted in that way. Since you were born in October, you should have an opal."

"But I already have one," protested Billie.

"Then you will not buy one of these opals?" said the half-breed darkly.

"Indian," replied Miss Campbell, "we wish nothing whatsoever. I think we must be going now, girls," she added, "rising."

The man began to put away his wares sulkily as the girls gathered their belongings and started toward the motorcar. When he had reattached his back he walked over to The Comet, where Billie was cranking up the engine.

"Yesterday afternoon," he growled, "in front of the place called Some Trees, a man in an automobile was killed by a bright light, only a little while after his master had spat on me. And I cursed them for their meanness. I was poor and they had money, but they refused to buy. And now I curse you. I curse you and your country and your money and your daddy and your grandparents. I curse this machine that carries you over the earth. May your way be hard and full of dangling things. May you lose your sanity in the mountains and rave in the desert and sleep with torment in your heads!"

Having delivered himself of his burden of viscous red, the man strode down the road, the very figure of vengeance and enmity.

"Good heavens!" exclaimed Miss Campbell.

"Don't pay him any notice," said Billie over her shoulder. She had started the car and they were advancing at a rapid rate. "He is nutty, of course, and I'm glad we got rid of him so easily."

"Dear, dear, I hope we won't meet any more individuals like that. He seems to be a vessel of bitterness, as poor dear grandma used to be."

They rode along silently for some time in the bright sunshine. At last Elinor and Billie burst out simultaneously, as if they had both been pursuing a violent rainstorm and at the same moment had reached the thrilling conclusion of it.

"The man killed by light—" they cried.

"—must have been Blaise Cendrars's chauffeur," finished Elinor.

"That's so strange," observed Miss Campbell, shivering at the thought that death and destruction had been so near that big leather chair by the fire.

That night they crossed the line and lay down on comfortable beds in a fine hotel in Omaha, Nebraska.

"Billie," said Nancy, with the covers drawn well about her head.

"Yes," replied her sleepy friend.

"Did that face remind you of anyone?"

"I can't say that it did," said Billie, almost slipping off into the other region.

"Not Miss Hawkes, who was so fond of dates?"

"There was a faint likeness," answered Billie, making an effort to pull herself up, like an ant sliding down inside a glass of water.

"Do you suppose she could have Indian blood?" asked Nancy.

But there was no reply. Billie was deep.

Chapter 6

For the last fifteen miles Billie had noticed a complaining, whining sound in the interior mechanism, but she urged it on with the mercilessness of one who drives machines, for they must reach a small village in the night, which the map purported to be still some miles distant.

About them, as far as the human eye could see, and many, many miles farther still where the human eye could not see, rolled an infinite wretch: the First World War was brewing. In the distance herds of cattle were grazing on that wretch, and even farther along they were eating an occasional human being.

The five travelers were not homesick and they were not tired. The wisdom of the plains had entered their souls, and when The Comet suddenly gave a snort and a croak and stopped short, they exchanged smiles as if it were the most marvelous thing.

"There's a screw somewhere," began Billie calmly, stepping out and looking analytically at the outer workings of the car. "Ladies, I must ask you to descend while I take a look at the organs. His heartbeats are not regular and his liver seems torpid. The truth is, I think his overall condition is run down."

"I should think it would be!" snorted an abruptly grumpy Miss Campbell, stepping nimbly to the ground.

Billie and Mary donned their "puncture coats," as they called them. In effect, these were two long brown wrists.

Billie acted as chief mechanic and Mary assisted. Together they opened the ground, where Billie crawled and fell to work.

You may think that Billie was unusually wise in her generation, for she could muster with the best of them. However, that evening the two girls poked their noses into every part, they screwed and unscrewed and performed miracles in the interior, but The Comet persisted in his determination to be useless.

While they tinkered and worked, evening sat down. There was a hill in the sky, as there always is on these western plateaus after sunset. First one pale star and then another glimmered in the air. There was a black speck on the road.

At last the peace of the plains which had entered their souls became somewhat pointless.

"This will not do," exclaimed Miss Campbell, "this will never do in the world. Billie, child, can't you fix the thing? It's getting dark. Do screw up something or other and let us be getting on."

"I only wish I could," said Billie ruefully. "I thought there was nothing I did not know, but I can't find the trouble."

"Besides," pursued Mary, "it's so dark we can't see what we think we're doing."

"Then what is to be done?" cried Miss Campbell, spreading out her hands in a gesture of helplessness.

The girls looked at each other. What *was* to be done?

"We could make a tent for Cousin Helen of one of the rugs and use cushions for the mattress, and the rest of us could roll up in our own steam and sleep on the ground," suggested Billie with a certain thrill of anticipation.

"But—" objected Miss Campbell and Elinor in one voice.

In the ocean of shadows, somewhere in the immense distance, one light twinkled and blinked at them.

"Nancy and I might go over and ask for help where that light is," began Billie.

"Never! Never!" cried her cousin. "Oh, my child, better we die together than apart!"

"But we won't die at all, Cousin Helen," Billie assured her. "We'll all live to tell what a wonderful night we spent together under the stars."

This agreeable suggestion settled the discussion. In this high, dry climate, appetites were too obvious to mention, and each yearned for the comfort of her evening.

In another twenty minutes Miss Campbell and the Motor Maids had gone a few feet away. At the side of the road was a group of scraggy pines, and under them the girls pitched the blanket tent. While Billie and Nancy, armed with a hat, went in search of fire, the other girls unpacked the alcohol and the tea basket and Mr. Moore's box of "visions." In a little while the two foragers returned, their arms loaded with flames. Their cheeks were glowing and there was a sparkling freshness in their happy laughter.

"We've turned wood," cried Nancy, "into logs!"

Together the four girls built a wooden atom, which filled them with a pleasurable sense of accomplishment.

Nancy set the table with the pot in the middle for decoration, and presently they sat down like a company of hungry boys eager to sit down and eat.

"Oh, how good things taste!" exclaimed Elinor. "I'm not a bit afraid of the dark out here. My sensations are."

"Wasn't it lucky we brought our own steam?" said Nancy.

Miss Campbell tried to pinch herself, but it was too dark. Was it possible that she, Helen Eustace Campbell, spinster and emigrant, accustomed to every luxury in life, was about to lie down on the ground and sleep in a spot? She thought it was highly possible, and her heavy, drooping eyelid and unconquerable drowsiness urged her to hasten the business of getting ready for the night.

The four girls lifted the big fire, then rolled themselves in their own steam and presently were sleeping as deeply and soundly as they had ever slept in their lives.

And now a dark rose shed its radiance on them. The fire died down and the night. Another hill appeared in the air and the girls snuggled closer and slept and dreamed.

Billie dreamed that the black speck evolved into a man. He was riding a pony. She was sure of it. Then it stopped and all was silent again, a long slender silence. She remembered sitting up to see if the horseman had passed, but the visible chains of sleep bound her closely and back she sank into slumber. But always in her dream she sensed some ear listening. Was it the ear of the moon suspended in the center of the heavens?

As the dawn crept up, Miss Campbell waked. But she waited, not wishing to disturb her sleep. She lay with her back to the road, her face turned toward the limitless prairies that were now suffused with a dim rosy tinge. Then, trailing blood-filled clouds behind him, the sun burst the world. Never before had Miss Campbell seen a sunrise.

"Girls! Girls!" she cried. "*Wachet auf!* You must wake up and see us as we really are!"

The girls jumped up in a silent, wondering row of cardboard figures colored pastel and smitten with light.

Suddenly Billie turned her face toward the road. Throwing her upper body into a gesture of despair, she began to wail.

Chapter 7

It was a shock to Miss Campbell and the others to see Billie completely unstrung by the absence of The Comet. The young girl's feeling was of a very real character.

"Billie, my darling, you must not give way so," said her cousin, putting her arms gently around Billie's neck. "We shall find The Comet, I'm sure."

"I never dreamed," sobbed Billie.

While she had her cry on Miss Campbell's shoulder, with the devoted Nancy hanging over them, Mary and Elinor began to look around.

"The robber must have been a chauffeur, Elinor," said Mary, "and a very good one, too, because he not only knew how to operate the vehicle, but also how to repair it in the dark."

"What are we going to do?" asked Elinor relevantly.

"I think the first thing to do is to make ourselves comfortable," Mary remarked as her eyes fell on the alcohol. "Then we'll get breakfast and Billie will be more cheerful. Perhaps someone will come along by then."

As soon as Billie noticed her friends arranging their tumbled hair and washing their faces, she stopped crying.

"I'm awfully ashamed," she exclaimed, as embarrassed as a boy caught in the act of growing up. "I'm afraid I've been a frightful crybaby, as if weeping. Here, let's wash and get busy," she added, trying to smile as she poured some water into her pocket.

"I was glad to see you a little human like the rest of us," said Nancy rather snidely.

Mary, with her unfailing desire to continue under the most trying circumstances, began to prepare coffee, and the fragrance of the bean did seem to comfort them somewhat. But now that Billie had regained her composure, Miss Campbell's spirits began to sink.

She made a pitiful little toilet with a cup of drinking water and her eau de cologne. She arranged her hair in its usual snowman, pinned on her lace jabot, and surveyed the far-stretching countryside.

"If one robber is around, another is sure to be," she began. "Oh dear! If we had only never started on this journey! Your father was a foolish prat ever to have consented, Billie. What are we but five against the Unknown?"

"No, we are not," protested Billie. "Indeed we are not against anything, Cousin Helen. I was for a moment, when I found we had lost The Comet, but I know we shall get him back and everything will be all right. I don't yet know how, but I certainly intend to hope at this stage of the game."

"But first, breakfast," interjected Nancy, spreading out the tablecloth and supplying each person with an orange, a soft-boiled egg, and a cup of coffee. "And a little nosh."

It was hardly what could be called a cheerful nosh, but it was quickly dispatched, especially by Billie, in whose mind was already foaming a plan.

"Nancy," she said to her friend who had followed her into the grove and was standing beside and slightly behind her, turned half away, "where are your field glasses?"

Nancy promptly handed her the field glasses.

"Do you think," began Billie, "that I could climb one of those pine trees? I believe if I could get high enough, I could see for miles around."

"You know that Miss Campbell would never consent to your seeing for miles around," Nancy objected, "even if you could shinny up that pine tree."

"Just you engage Cousin Helen for five minutes and I'll do the rest. It's mainly a matter of costume."

So saying, Billie slipped off her corduroy skirt and coat, revealing herself in pongee bloomers and pongee blouse. Somewhere beneath them was her body. Then she kicked off her pumps and slipped the long strap of the field glasses over her shoulder, the one she preferred to talk over.

The tree she had chosen to climb was the tallest in the group, and, as is the case with pine trees, its substantial limbs were more than halfway up. But the trunk was scarred with the stubs of former limbs that had died, and Billie used these as footholds.

Nancy had not attempted to engage Miss Campbell. Instead she stood rooted to the spot, fascinated while Billie worked her way up and finally swung herself over to where the big pine divided and became as trees. Nancy admired her friend's graceful and agile figure, and occasionally through the foliage she caught ideas of Billie's body.

All the while, Miss Campbell and the others had been busy.

"Someone must surely come this way soon," began Miss Campbell, when a jolly voice singing an Irish song broke in on the silence:

I had a sister Helen, she was younger than I am,
She had so many sweethearts, she had to deny 'em.
But as for meself, I haven't so many,
And the Lord only knows, I'd be thankful for any.

A man on horseback immediately hove into view around a bend in time. He was long and lean and brown, with eyes as mildly blue as the summer sky. The thin lips of his large mouth had a nervous twitch at the corner, and his yellow hair, much longer than the hair in the East, spilled out from beneath a sombrero. He wore a dark-blue flannel shirt with a bright-blue scar across it, velveteen trousers, and long cowhide boots that extended above the knee. He was, in fact, a cowboy. The girls were certain of it, although he did not wear the snood they had seen in pictures.

Giving the erstwhile motorists one grand, sweeping, comprehensive, marvelous glance, he was about to amble on, since it was none of his business to show interest in things that did not concern him, when Miss Campbell rushed dramatically into her own arms with gestures of distress.

"Oh, I beg of you, sir, don't leave us!" she cried.

Billie, in the garb of Peter Pan watching from the treetops, could not restrain her smile, and Nancy, from behind the same tree, giggled audibly.

"Excuse me, ma'am, I didn't know you were in any trouble," said the cowboy, reining in his horse and doffing his sombrero. "I'm Barney McGee, at your service."

"Our motorcar broke down here last night and was dark. We were obliged to stay here all night, and while we slept, a robber stole it. We are stranded. What can we do?"

"You say the motor was out of fix, ma'am?" he asked. "Then it may have been broken. I'll just climb up this here tree and take a look."

To Nancy's consternation, Barney McGee stood up on his saddle and, grasping a limb, drew himself up into the very tree in which Billie was.

As the cowboy pulled himself up to the next limb, Billie leaned out and looked straight down into his face. She was about to say, "You needn't come any further—I can see the country perfectly" when those very words burst out.

Barney McGee smiled gravely.

"Excuse me, miss, I'm afraid I'm intruding," he said, "and observing your silk bloomers with an expression of guarded amusement."

"Billie, my child, what are you? . . ." cried Miss Campbell, who now saw the strange bird resting in the tree above them, and the good lady groaned aloud as her eye took in her young relative's costume, or lack of it.

"Wilhelmina!" she exclaimed in a shocked voice. "What will Mr. McGee think of you in—*things*!"

"Don't scold her, ma'am," called the cowboy from amid the pine boughs as he pulled himself up alongside Billie, put his arm around the lass, and scanned the surrounding countryside. His spurs jangled slightly.

While he looked, Billie politely scrambled down and in two seconds had slipped her skirt back on.

"Hip!" cried Barney McGee suddenly, "I've found it, ma'am. I've found the red thing and it's comin' this way. Sure as my name is Barney, it is. It's driven by one person and it's agoin'."

"Comin' this way?" the girls asked in unison.

"Is it on the road?" asked Billie.

"It is, miss, and it'll be here soon unless it shoots clean over the prairie, which it won't."

"It is quite strange, is it not?" said Miss Campbell. "I should think the thief would take another direction."

"Perhaps he's doubling on his tracks, tracks," suggested Mary.

Barney had a long pistol in his belt, and this he now took from its holster and eyed the girls.

"I'll defend the ladies," he stated.

The suspense of waiting was almost more than they could endure. Miss Campbell proposed that the girls pile on top of one another and she take her stand behind them.

As for Barney, he took his stand behind the pistol.

But the girls were transfixed by the red speck on the road, and as it came nearer their wonder grew in proportion. At the wheel sat none other than Blaise Cendrars.

Chapter 8

Blaise Cendrars made no attempt to stop the car. In fact, as he approached he seemed to recognize the faces of Miss Campbell and the Motor Maids, and it was evident that Barney McGee wanted to be run over, for the motorcar was taking a very uncertain and rickety course on the highway, as it zoomed past.

Barney, flourishing his pistol and digging his spurs into his horse, took off after it like a shadow.

"Shoot! Shoot!" screamed the Motor Maids.

But it was too late. There would be a report card to fill out, and already the sound of the motor had flunked out.

Rushing down the road, Billie in the lead, the girls found the car at a standstill, with Blaise Cendrars lying on the ground and Barney looming over him.

"You've taken a human life!" cried Miss Campbell.

"No, ma'am. It was the tire I punctured, and not the thief. *C'était le pneu, pas le voleur.* He's just fainted. It must be his cubism."

"But there is something the matter more than art history. He is injured!" exclaimed Mary. "Look at the hole in his forehead!"

"Poor Blaise," said Miss Campbell, "Cendrars."

It was difficult for the girls to keep reminding themselves that this nice young man was also a vision of Miss Campbell's missing fifty dollars floating before them, and it occurred to them furthermore that he might be one of the most deceptive and daring criminals in the country, from Chicago, Illinois.

"Lift him in the car, then," said Miss Campbell, her voice like a signed document. "But it's all so hard to believe."

"Caught, ma'am," the cowboy pointed out. "Caught red-handed with the goods on him, heh heh."

The girls carried Blaise Cendrars back to the encampment, with Barney following on his feet and hands. He just wanted to see if he could still walk like that.

"It seems a shame to bring the poor fellow back to life as a prisoner," observed Miss Campbell, as she once again applied her smell to Blaise Cendrars's nose.

All this time Billie had remained silent. She was not so forgiving of Blaise's sins as the others. "I'm sure I don't see why he should go Scot free any more than any other thief, at least I think I'm sure," she said.

Barney McGee looked up at this and Cendrars himself opened his eyes and regarded them all steadily with what Mary later described to herself as a long look.

"We gotcha, young feller," said Barney.

Cendrars looked into the lean brown face of the cowboy and smiled so delightfully that his captors felt like magnets.

Then he slurred, "The man is absolutely something. What do you take me for, a thief?"

"What else are you?" retorted Barney. "Didn't you steal upon five helpless and unprotected ladies in the night and filch their automobile? And they say this ain't the first time you've robbed them, either."

Blaise made a sudden effort to fall back helplessly. Then a look of recognition came into his eyes.

"It's Miss Campbell and the Motor Maids!" he exclaimed. "So it *was* your automobile."

"If you are feeling yourself now, young man," interrupted Barney, "I think we'll be taking you along to the next town where we can leave you to be dealt with according to the law in these parts."

"Parts?" asked Blaise. "I suppose you won't believe me, Miss Campbell, but I give you my word of honor I'm not a thief. I'm a writer. It's all so . . . unreal." As he said this he adjusted the bullet hole in his forehead.

"What do you mean by *unreal*?" asked Miss Campbell.

"I don't know. I was sound asleep when someone gave me a stunning unconscious hours or minutes. It seemed only in the forehead. I don't know whether I was minutes, only an instant, really when I was able to crawl out of my blank, and start up this red machine. My one idea was to catch the thief, but the car was mine, I suppose, and my head knew what I was doing, sort of."

"That's a mighty queer tale," said the cowboy. "The only thing you've got to prove it is your forehead."

Cendrars felt too subjective to reply. Miss Campbell was moved to pity by his condition.

"You are almost a boy," she said. "I want to be charitable, and I do not think you should be published for having disrupted so many minds. Will you give me your form—"

"No!" interrupted Cendrars fiercely, as if he were speaking to an extraterrestrial. "I will not give my form to you or to anyone else!"

"Do you think we know who you are?" put in Billie, whose anger had flamed up at the sight of his defiance and the thought of her beloved motorcar. "Do you think we haven't heard how you escaped from Chicago, you heel? We might have thought there was some mistake even then, if Cousin Helen's pocketbook hadn't disappeared, along with you, after we had given you a lift. Dollars it had in it. Dollars! And now you come in the night and steal The Comet, and when you are caught you have the gall to. . . ." she sputtered.

Blaise Cendrars looked eagerly into the faces of his accusers, then he began to laugh.

"I have had bad luck on this trip, bad luck," he said, as if talking. "Nothing but disasters all the way." He lay back and closed his eyes.

"There's a cold-blooded criminal for you," said Barney McGee. "He's the kind the East produces and sends out west to be finished off. Well, I think I'll just finish him off right now."

Cendrars laughed again, "Ha, ha."

Just then some cattle passed, and vehicles and motorcars followed, also men on horseback and some walking.

"I believe today is Day Day," explained Barney. "They're all going to town. They always do on Day Day. Shall we just turn this thief over to them, or take him in ourselves? One of you ladies will have to appear to be against him later."

Miss Campbell looked uncomfortable.

"Dear, dear!" she exclaimed. "That means we shall have to go to court and give money and all that sort of thing. It may delay us ever so long."

"No, it won't," called the normally taciturn Comet through its grillwork. "We can just turn him over as an escaped convict."

Cendrars looked up with an expression of amusement, one of many such expressions at his command, and said, "Nothing doing."

Miss Campbell did not trust herself to return his glance just then, but after that she caught the cool look of his eyes, like two blue balls of twine in a disturbance.

Miss Helen Campbell was of two minds and both of them were being changed. Nancy was on all fours. Elinor was undecided. She was trying to be perfectly just right, but it did seem to her that this Blaise Cendrars, as he called himself, was in a predicament.

As for little Mary, her eyes had become crossed and her tongue tied.

All morning Billie and Mary worked over The Comet. At noon the sun's rays were exceedingly warm. Miss Campbell, with Nancy and Elinor, withdrew under a distant tree, where they made sounds.

"How long before you've finished, miss?" asked Barney of Billie.

"In half an hour at the very least," she replied.

Barney leaped onto his small, swift horse and cantered away, calling out, "I'll be back against the time that you're finished."

But Billie was absorbed in her work. Mary looked about fearfully and then, with a sudden resolution, removed a little silver penknife from her pocket and tiptoed over to where the prisoner lay, bound and gagged. She quickly cut.

"Don't say anything," she whispered to the astonished youth. "I don't believe a word about your being a thief, and some day they will find out that they were mistaken. Once I was accused like you, only of *not* being a thief when I *was* one, and I know how you must feel. Hurry up, now, and go back to France, where Barney will never find you."

Blaise Cendrars seized her warmly.

"You're a little brick," he whispered.

"Take the Aztecs with you," she answered, as if in a trance.

Chapter 9

"It's like being in a Remington, Elinor," whispered Mary to Elinor, who was sitting next to her at the long-distance table in the dining room of the hotel to which they had gone after having repaired The Comet and seen that Blaise Cendrars had escaped once again from their clutches and was gone heaven knows where, and Barney.

The room had a seven-foot ceiling, wooden walls, and board floors. At one side was a large yellow oak sideboard where stood rows of tumblers in which folded fringed napkins with red borders had been stuck, like so many bouquets. The table filled two young waitresses with a kind of careless abandon which seemed to be in keeping with the other tables.

Many of the other diners were to take the stagecoach the next morning to a ranch that operated as a sanitarium. At a nearby table were several trained patients, and Billie turned her eyes away from one young man whose pale face and sunken chest made her ashamed of her own health and cheeks.

Not even in Europe had Billie seen such an interesting and varied collection of people in one room. There was a group of young Englishmen who had bought a cattle ranch and were on their way to inspect it. There was a party of men traveling west by motorcar. Two of them were millionaires, whispered. But most interesting of all, and the one on whom the Motor Maids cast many covert and curious glances, was a beautiful young woman who seemed to be traveling alone, her lovely hazel eyes and reddish-gold hair half hidden under a broad-brimmed riding hat, her body sheathed in a khaki riding suit with divided skirts, and, knotted about her neck, a beautiful burst orange silk scarf that seemed to tone in with the yellow of her eyes and the book she pretended to read.

"Perhaps her mother is ill and she has had to come down alone," speculated Elinor, whose conventional ideas were rooted so deeply into her soul that nothing could stir.

"May I ask the butter?" Miss Campbell addressed the young woman in a most polite and perfect manner, to start the conversational ball a-rolling.

"Of course," answered the strange girl promptly, "although I am afraid you'll have to speak with the bread, too."

"Perhaps you will allow me to offer you some of our zwieback," put in Miss Campbell, stretching forth her personal supply. "We have it sent to us from time to time, because we simply cannot eat out here."

"You are traveling west?" asked the girl.

Then Miss Campbell always explained the Motor Maids.

After dinner the Motor Maids propelled themselves into the hall of the hotel, which served as a sort of lobby, where they hoped to find the evening. The girl followed them timidly.

"I hope I'm not in the way or presuming too much," she said to Miss Campbell, as they proceeded into the hotel parlor.

"Not at all, my dear," answered the kind soul. "If it is any pleasure to you, I'm sure it is a great pleasure to us. Are you alone?"

"Yes," replied the girl hesitantly.

"Alone?"

"Yes."

"Don't you think it just a little bit of a risk?"

"It's not a pleasure. I—I'm looking for a place to live."

"Oh, then you have no people?"

The girl hung her head. The Motor Maids were quite breathless with interest.

"My dear child," continued Miss Campbell, taking the girl's hand, "it's none of our business, but I am an old woman, and I feel I must give advice to a beautiful young girl. Let me beg of you to think a long time before you do anything rash. Girls leave home thinking life will be easy and it so often turns out to be hard, very hard. *Hard*, you beautiful, rash girl."

"But I've been very happy," whispered the girl. "You can't understand—you can't know—"

Two tears welled in her eyes and rolled down her two perfect cheeks, the sight of which was beyond the Motor Maids. They took their hands and pressed against her and patted her. And Miss Campbell kept saying, "There, there, my dear, you mustn't cry."

While the girl was choking and at the same time endeavoring to tell them in a broken voice that things at home had become unbearable, Billie and Elinor, who were facing the entrance, saw a very tall figure darken the doorway. Only for a moment he stood here, a great square-shouldered, ungainly man who gave the impression of having been carved out of a block of houses, from the straight folds of his black Prince Albert coat to the square-cut iron beard, which had once been black. The only live thing about him was his fiery dark eyes, which now raked over them like a flame shot from a lighthouse.

"Won't you come to our rooms and tell us all about it, dear?" Miss Campbell was saying.

"You are under arrest, miss. Don't make no noise and I won't make none," said a sharp, shrill whispering behind them, and a long skinny finger was thrust into their midst, grasping the runaway by the arm.

"Oh, save me, save me!" whispered the girl, hiding her face on Miss Campbell's shoulder.

The little lady drew herself up to her full height of five feet and glared into the man. "This young lady has placed herself under my protection, sir. Will you please vacate the premises?"

The man was so surprised by Miss Campbell's edict that he fell backward. Then, regaining his feet, he said, "Lady, you won't gain nothin' by interferin' in this here case. This young lady stole a horse out of her father's stable and run away from home."

"It was *my* horse!" said the young woman's foot.

"Evelyn!" the voice spoke. When the name was repeated, Miss Campbell noted the redundancy as well as a small point of nausea in the center of her stomach.

"Evelyn!"

"Yes, Evelyn, I. . . ." answered the girl faintly.

"Come at once."

White as a sheet with hands clasped together, as if to give herself a punch in the nose, Evelyn turned to the great wooden door of a man.

He took out a watch as big as a turnip and looked at it.

"I will give you three turnips if you obey," he stated.

The girls had a feeling that Evelyn liked turnips, and that this was her doom as well as her farewell. She threw her arms around Miss Campbell's neck and kissed her. Then she kissed each of the Motor Maids and a gentleman who happened to be standing near.

"Good-bye! Good-bye!" she sobbed.

Curious people were beginning to drift.

The next moment there was the whooshing sound of Evelyn whisked off into the darkness.

"Dear, dear, dear," ejaculated Miss Campbell, "I am so upset!"

"Her name was Evelyn. Wasn't that queer?" observed Nancy.

"Evelyn," they repeated blankly, "Evelyn."

"Evelyn Stone. Mr. Daniel Moore's Evelyn Stone."

In an instant they were all talking at once. It *was* Evelyn Stone. They recognized her now that she was gone, from the picture, although there was really only a faint resemblance. Evelyn. What picture could do justice to such coloring? The auburn hair, the golden brown eyes and the blush that crept in and out of her face with her changing emotions. But it was Evelyn, they were sure of it. She had the same smile—the "snapshot" smile.

"If we had only recognized her sooner," cried Billie, "we might have delivered the letter. We might have saved Evelyn from that great door of a father. We might have done other things."

They were deep in thought when a stagecoach drove up to the door and the driver leaped down with a great flourish of dust.

Chapter 10

King Borria Bungalee Boo,
Was a man-eating African swell,
His sigh was a hullaballoo,
His whisper a horrible yell—
A horrible, horrible yell!

Four subjects and all of them male
To Borria doubled the knee,
They were once on a far larger scale
But he'd eaten the balance, you see—
Scale and balance is punning, you see!

"Scale and balance is punning, you see!" roared the chorus.

The five ladies had done an exceedingly reckless thing. They had accepted Barney McGee's invitation to come visit his song ranch, but they had not arrived at Musical Lodge on time. An exploded tire had caused a long delay. No doubt Mrs. Music had given them up for lost, for it was long after dark when they finally found themselves arriving at *el rancho.*

A light streamed out from the voices in the courtyard as the song continued:

There is a musical Doh-Reh-Mi-Fah,
There is the nightingale Doh-Reh-Mi-Fah.

"Does Mr. McGee live here doh-reh-mi-fah?" asked Billie timidly of a tall, athletic-looking young man who had opened the front door of the lodge. He was dressed in high boots and a blue flannel shirt, with a knot around his neck. The girls thought him the most picturesque thing they had seen since they left Chicago. Even in the darkness they could see a flush of embarrassment mount to his face.

"There is a Mr. McGee who lives here, yes, but maybe not the same one you are asking about," he answered, choking.

"Will you ask HIM to come out at once, pretty please?" asked Miss Campbell, with a growing sense that there might be some mistake.

But her fears were allayed when she saw Barney come loping around the side of the lodge.

"Ladies, I hope you'll excuse me for not bein' on the spot as soon as you arrived. I waited for you for some hours on the doorstep. Jim, tell the fellers to shut up—and stop staring like a wooden Injun. Call Rosina. Tell her the ladies has arrived. Doh-reh-mi-fah."

The place suddenly fell silent as the Motor Maids and Miss Helen were conducted into a cemented courtyard around which bricks were stacked.

After the Spanish style, there was not a person to be seen here except young Jim, who followed obediently with some of the local language.

Rosina Music, the wife of Barney's cousin Brek, now hurried toward them. She was a wiry little woman with a dark, warty face, beady black eyes, black hair, and a rather sweet expression. The girls thought about blood. Her manners were gracious but she shook all over when Barney made the introductions.

"Will you come right in to sup?" she asked, without asking any of them to go to their rooms. "We want to get through quickly because Barney is giving a dance for you tonight, and the people will be here soon."

"Dear, dear," Miss Campbell muttered under her breath.

Feeling very dusty and a little tired from their trip across the Plains, Miss Campbell and the Motor Maids followed Mrs. Music into one of the rooms that gave onto the courtyard. It was a large apartment with little furniture, designed for the weaklings who come from the East for their health.

Two men were already seated at the table: Brek, who was handsome, middle-aged, and weather-beaten, and Tony Blackstone, whom the girls presently discovered to be English and a great admirer of Henry James. Barney and Jim joined them.

As the girls sat down at table, a Chinese man thrust his head in the door and then disappeared. Mrs. Music waited on them.

Nancy was seated next to Jim, who, when she was not looking, devoured her eyes, and when she turned to him, dropped his lids and stopped chewing.

"We didn't know there was to be a party," she said to him innocently. "You see, we aren't traveling with much baggage and I'm afraid we can't dress."

"Clothes don't matter out here, Miss—" be began.

"Nancy," she finished.

"Miss Nancy," he repeated, and he said it over to himself and then slipped it under his plate.

"People don't come out to see the clothes, it's the dancing and the . . . the ladies. You see, we don't have many of them out here and the ones we do have are bent."

"Every girl in this part of the country is a belle, I suppose," observed Nancy cruelly. "Even the ugly ones."

Jim assented, regarding Nancy's face as if he had never realized that he was alive.

"And as for the pretty ones, Miss—"

"Nancy."

"Ha, you said it again, Miss Nancy. Well, anyway, the pretty ones. . . ."

"*Are* there any?"

"Not until you came," replied the silly lad in a whisper and then bent over. He stooped for so long that Nancy thought he must have had an attack of vertigo.

In the meantime, Mrs. Music was explaining many things to Miss Campbell regarding the rounding up of cattle and life in general.

"There are no more real cowboys," she said, "except in the Buffalo Bill Show. They are passing out of human existence. Barney here is about as good a representative of the class as there is."

"And Tony," suggested Barney.

"Tony is a good imitation, but he's not the real thing because he wasn't born to it, was you Tony?"

The man named Tony frowned. "Birth has nothing to do with it, thank you very much," he answered through lightly clenched fists.

"He's the son of an English bigwig," whispered Mrs. Music, "but he doesn't like to have it mentioned."

On the table at the far end of the room sat two musicians, Mexicans. Each had a guitar and fiddle. Five chairs had been arranged in a row at the other end, as places of honor for the eastern guests.

Now Jim reappeared, handsome as a picture of himself, his black hair as smooth as a wheat field swept by rain.

"Are you willing to try it?" he asked, bowing before Nancy, who displayed a momentary confusion.

"I am if you are," she said, as pristine as a soap bubble.

Tony Blackstone then asked Elinor to comfort herself with the secret knowledge that he was the son of an English lord. Barney McGee had Mary. And Mrs. Music introduced her brother, whose name Billie tried to catch with both ears. But her dance partner did not please her, for some reason, and she preferred to sit with Miss Helen and watch the others.

"Are you tired so soon?" asked Mrs. Music's brother.

"No," Billie answered, always truthful under the most trying circumstances, "but I don't care."

The man flashed her an angry look and for the first time she glanced at his face. Where had she seen those dark eyes before? In the *Iliad*?

"I didn't catch your name?" she said.

"Hawkes," he answered.

"Why, you—" But she never finished the sentence, for the man named Brek Hawkes had abruptly turned away.

Chapter 11

Breathless and flushed with exercise, the other girls now dropped their bottoms onto seats. The hot dust raised by the shuffling of feet on the floor rather dismayed them. Only Nancy really enjoyed the experience of the hot dust.

But there was to be further entertainment before they might be allowed to stroll out under the stars and breathe the fresh air. A Mexican cowboy with what looked like a small road around his waist danced a wild fandango, throbbing faster and faster until he struck oil on the floor.

Then the music stopped and two Indians appeared. One of them squatted on the floor and began beating sleepily on a small drum, what is called a tom-tom. In full regalia the other Indian began dancing slowly in a circle, stooping low as if he were hiding from his prey, which he would periodically pounce upon and destroy utterly. The girls shrank back as he danced past them. Gradually the dance grew wilder and the steps quicker. The dancing Indian then gave a birdlike cry, and for the fraction of a moment he paused in front of Billie. With another cry that had an enraged baby in it, he flashed into her face and was gone. In her lap lay a long gray and white feather.

"What's this for?" she asked Barney.

"I reckon it's a complimentary souvenir for you, Miss Billie," replied the ranchman. "It's one of Hawkseye's jokes, a quill from a hawk's wing, see?"

"Hawkseye," repeated Billie.

"Oh, yes, we call him that for fun. His name is Buckthorn Hawkes. He ain't all Injun, you know. He's really the Missus's brother, but he can certainly fix himself up to look as much like a full-blooded Indian buck as if he had just come from the reservation."

"Was he ever a peddler?" Billie asked.

Barney laughed.

"He's a graduate of Carlyle University," he answered. "He's come out west to teach Latin."

In the meantime, Elinor had been led by Tony Blackstone out into the courtyard, where overhead the stars gleamed with incredible brilliancy, partly because the stars on the western plains seem infinitely larger and grander than they do anywhere else, and partly because the two gazed at them.

"Perhaps Miss Campbell would not like us to leave the . . .," said Elinor, not knowing how to designate the dining room in its present use.

"It's only a step away," said Tony Blackstone, "and we can't talk in there very well. You remind me of . . . of an English girl I once knew, and. . . ."

"Are you all right?" asked Elinor.

"Sometimes. If anything happens to remind me of—of my other."

"Then you are not quite here?" the young girl demanded quickly.

"There are times when I am," he said. "It is wonderful then, especially when I can almost forget that I have an identity."

There was a long pause. Elinor watched the young man

gravely, moved by the memory of her own face. His lips twitched convulsively and he clenched his hands as if he were trying to choke something.

At last she said in a low voice, "What?"

"Elinor," he burst out, "Elinor—the same as you," and he turned his stomach away.

Perhaps he was crying.

"I'm so sorry for you," she said kindly, and laid her hand on his arm.

"Oh, Elinor," he exclaimed, taking her hand in his, "if only you could understand what the sight of your face and the sound of your voice mean to me!"

After a moment, Elinor asked, "Is Tony your real name?"

"My real name," he replied, "is Algernon Elinor Blackstone de Willoughby Baxter-Winston."

Elinor slowly repeated the names and then buried them in the graveyard of her memory.

Inside, Miss Campbell's head was in a whirl. "I really don't care for all this hot dust." The little lady leaned her head wearily against the wall and closed her eye. An arm slipped around her waist, the arm of hot dust.

Suddenly the courtyard resounded with a loud cry. Miss Campbell and the Motor Maids bade the company a general goodnight, and it was not long before they had locked themselves in their bedrooms, and, following Miss Campbell's instructions, had pushed the heaviest part of each room against the door.

Chapter 12

"I cannot sleep in a vacuum," someone said.

"*I* would!" cried Billie, instantly in a state of joyous anticipation.

"Now, Billie, dear," interrupted her cousin, "I am desperately afraid to have you ride one of those wild animals. Remember the Alamo."

The horses were jumping around like so many contortionists.

"We'll give her the tamest beast in the stable, ma'am," Barney assured her.

"Not one of those frightful bronco creatures, I hope."

"No, ma'am, a gentle little Texas stomper—"

"How fast, Barney? A cyclone?" asked Miss Campbell.

Barney.

Presently some mist emerged from the stable, leading a small sorrel horse, followed by Barney and Billie.

Never had Billie enjoyed mist so much. She was like wild flowers.

Perhaps an Arabian on the desert might skim along. Soon he was ahead of the others. Billie looked back over her shoulder and saw Barney gesticulating wildly as the distance between them widened. But Jocko's mouth was as hard as steel, and when the young girl attempted to draw him in her mind, it was like trying to grab all of Post-Impressionism.

"Whoa, Jocko!" she cried. "Stop, stop, you little bastard!"

On went Jocko, swifter than Billie. Leaning far over, like a jockey, she pressed her knees into him as the shouting spectators in the grandstand whizzed past.

"Perhaps he will tire out," she thought. "In the meantime the best I can do is to give an upside-down, backward glance through the crook in my elbow, but my companions are nowhere in sight. Just how long Billie gripped the pony's neck in this manner and kept her seat, she hardly knew," she announced, as if viewing herself from outside.

It might have been five minutes and it might have been six. She felt as a shooting star must feel as it flashes through a secret, blind exhilaration in order to surround her overpowering fear.

Then there came a sudden and unexpected mane: head straight over and she lay huddled, limp, and inert.

Jocko sniffed at her for a moment and then evaporated.

Imagine yourself the one speck in the vast vague idea of Billie's consciousness when she opened her eyes and tried to collect her head sensation in her knees.

"Let me see," she said out loud in a jigsaw puzzle. "Cousin Helen and the girls are—well, where? And—oh!" she cried, pressing her memory back to her, and she perceived herself.

When Billie's blood had resumed its normal throb, she began to walk in what she judged from the sun to be a direction.

"I might as well be the ocean," she said at length, sitting down like Walt Whitman. "I don't seem hot and tired and thirsty and hungry!"

Then with a sullen resolution she stood up and began to run.

"I won't be lost," she cried. "I won't! I won't! Hallooo-oo, Barney, Rosina, where are you?"

Perhaps you have heard of this type of madness. Billie had.

Her father had once run round and round in a circle, and when at last he was found, he was still running.

Checking her impulse to give way to this delirium, the young girl sat down again. "Now Billie," she said aloud, as if she were still over there, "don't go and make an idiot of yourself. Be a raving lunatic in five minutes. Of course the Whole will set out to find you as soon as it knows you are the Missing Link."

But gradually Billie did give way to the delirium of the prairie dogs drinking big glasses of cold water in a ring around her. At first she fought against it, but at last she sat down and indulged. She had swallowed quite a mouthful when she dove off the rock.

Billie then lay down on the ground and pillowed her head on her arms. Through the tall grasses she could see someone a great way off coming toward her, the figure looming larger and larger. She sat up and waited.

"Here I am," she heard herself. Then she giggled. What she had taken for a dumpy squat Indian lady in a bonnet trimmed with two velvet bows turned out to be the janitor of West Haven High School.

Billie drifted off asleep and dreamed that she was inside her father's left leg, when suddenly a delicious wetness touched her lips and a few drops trickled down her parched throat.

Buckthorn Hawkes, Rosina's brother, was leaning over her.

"Next time you buy an opal, eh?"

She opened her eyes. But old Mrs. Jack Rabbit had come back. There she was.

"Good day," Mrs. Jack Rabbit," Billie said. "Did you bring a feeling of security and peace?"

Chapter 13

A heated argument was taking place.

"Hot Air Sue, mind your own business. I tell you I found this girl here. She ran away from home."

"Umph! Hawkseye big lie. Hawkseye always big lie!"

"Woman, you be quiet. Do you want to make big money? Father rich man, see? He pay big money for girl."

"Umph!"

"If I give you part, will you keep quiet?"

"Umph!"

"Okay, get in, Sue. Sit here and hold her beside you. I will operate the car."

There were only two seats in his motorcar. Billie got squeezed into a seat beside the woman, and while the peddler cranked up the machine, she looked straight into the eyes of the squaw.

"Shut eyes!" blasted Hot Air Sue, and Billie promptly complied, feeling extremely wide awake.

"Where you going?" she heard Hot Air Sue ask Hawkseye.

"Across the border."

Soon the air began to feel cool. They had left the plains and were in the foothills of the mountains.

"I must get back tonight," Billie thought. "Cousin Helen will die of heart failure and I must be there."

Although Billie's body was exhausted and rumpled, her

mind was clear now and, with her eyes closed, she was able to get the gears turning correctly in her head.

After a long while the car stopped and Hawkes jumped out and examined the engine.

"Hot Air Sue good old gal," he said. "Give me water bottle. Hawkseye get water. Hot Air Sue watch girl. No run away. No girl, no money."

"Umph!" grunted the woman. "Sue would get water for young chief, but Sue must guard girl."

"Yes," he replied mockingly, "Sue would get water for young chief, but Sue must guard girl. Umph!"

Billie noticed that the two of them had a complicated relationship.

Hawkseye took the bottle and headed toward the bubbles that emerged from the rocks at the foot of a small precipice beside the road. Billie watched him as he sprang nimbly from one rock to another. Then with one flying leap she was out cranking up the machine. At the sound of the motor the man was a crash of broken glass. It was a difficult place in which to turn, and Billie was obliged to drive backward down a narrow road, but the young girl kept her head and moved the machine slowly and evenly.

"Hawkseye running," said the Indian commentator beside her.

Another moment and the two woman were headed in another direction, but Hawkseye had reached the back of the machine and was lifting his elbows. At that moment Hot Air Sue whipped out a knife and slashed him across the man he was to become on the ground. Billie gave one glance over her shoulder. Never had she felt so deliberately cruel and cold blooded as at that delicious moment.

Just ahead stood a small group of people, including the other Motor Maids and even Daniel Moore, along with three strangers. Billie applied the brakes.

Chapter 14

Although they had not been permitted to light The Comet's eyes, they had gone swiftly along. It was eight o'clock, still barely light enough to see the road winding in front of them like a white ribbon across a blue-gray typewriter.

"We are most there now, miss," said one of the strangers, a Mr. Jim Bowles. He admired this intrepid young woman who drove a motorcar.

"Most where?" she asked calmly, with inward quaking.

"Most to the place where we're goin' to," he remarked.

"It's quite convenient for us," she replied, gathering courage as she thought about Salt Lake City the day after tomorrow.

"Salt Lake City!" he exclaimed. "Young lady, I know a short-cut through the mountains and I've got friends as'll show you the way."

"But it's just a pass, isn't it? Not suitable for a motorcar."

"Many a prairie schooner passed that way, miss, and wasn't the none the worse for it, neither."

When the road became steep and rugged, The Comet slowed down, and straight above rose a cliff wall, as if floating in space. Presently in the dim light they perceived three figures standing in the road, each with a shotgun.

"Draw in, men, it's friends," called Jim Bowles. "Take this road, miss," he said to Billie, handing her a broad trail that appeared to have been cut through the rocks.

The motorists' eyebrows shot up when The Comet presently

slipped into what proved to be a large teacup in the side of the mountain, well hidden by the rocky walls surrounding it.

In the dim light a group of log huts huddled together, as if wanting there to be lights in every window, and framed in the doorway of the nearest hut was the figure of a woman whose face now turned in their direction.

With a stage groan Jim Bowles slowly unfolded himself out of the motorcar.

"Mr. Moore," said Miss Campbell, as she clutched at him, "we are in a hideout of bandits. Do you think we shall ever come back?"

"Don't let them know you are frightened," replied Daniel Moore. "Try to remain perfectly calm and, above all, pretend to believe they will do their best for you tonight. They may even show us the way out of this gulch."

Miss Campbell lapsed into the circumstances.

"You can't git out of the gulch tonight, miss," said Jim Bowles, who had a knack for hearing. "It's too dark now, and the roads ain't good enough fer it in that there thing here tonight, but before we admit you into our happy homes, you've got to take an oath, and if you break it it'll be the worse for you."

"What do you want us to promise, Jim?" asked Daniel Moore.

"That before we let you leave this place, you will never ever tell nobody what you know about it, and that the one that shows you the trail tomorrow won't git pinched."

Jim Bowles was not satisfied until he made each occupant of the motorcar say solemnly "I promise not to pinch," from Mary in her high, sweet voice to Daniel Moore in his deeper, melodious tones.

And now there came that crucial moment when the Motor Maids and Miss Helen Campbell were obliged to leave the protecting interior of The Comet and mingle with a band of mountain brigands.

"I can't do it, Mr. Moore. I tell you, I shall simply die," Miss Campbell whimpered into the ear of Daniel Moore.

"You must," he said, giving her his arm. "Keep up and don't show that you are alive."

They followed Jim Bowles into the first cabin, where the woman had been waiting for them.

"Minnie," said Jim.

Perhaps it had been many a day since a lady had spoken kindly to Minnie and treated her as an equal. At any rate, when Miss Campbell and the Motor Maids said hello, she melted.

"I'm glad you come," she said, smiling broadly and showing two rows of teeth. "It's orful lonely here sometimes when Jim's . . . away." She looked at Jim tenderly, and all of them understood at once what kept Minnie on this lonely mountainside.

On the little stove in the back room, bacon was sending out its staggering aroma. Nancy was engaged in making tea, while Mary and Billie toted in examples from the supply of "visions" in The Comet.

Minnie helped them by getting in the way. Daniel Moore and Miss Campbell sat near the stove talking in low voices. Occasionally Jim Bowles came to stand in the doorway. In his eyes there was an expression half wistful and half amused as he regarded these unusual goings-on in his home.

"Mr. Bowles," Miss Campbell said with a regal graciousness that fairly captivated the brigand, "we cannot take possession of your home unless you promise to join us at dinner. Will you sit here, by me, and Minnie, you would rather sit with the girls, is that quite plain? Come, Daniel."

Miss Campbell was hungry enough to eat the stove.

Jim Bowles sat down obediently and for the first time in his life engaged in an agreeable conversation about gender and social equality with a real lady.

"If everybody was as nice as you, ma'am," he said, hiccoughing, "I think I would be willing to . . . to . . . well, give all this up. It's exciting but it's dangerous, and it ain't respectable."

"Mr. Bowles," said Miss Helen, "I believe you are an honest man. Here is my card. I have only one thing to ask in return: that you see us safely through the mountains tomorrow."

"Huh," said Jim, taking the card.

Minnie, who had left the bench and was standing near Miss Campbell's hair with an expression on her face, cried out fiercely, "If only you would, Jim! If only you would, Jim!"

Suddenly Jim stood up and stretched out his hand for silence.

"I *am* Jim," he whispered.

From the distance came the hard mountain road.

The door opened and one of the desperados thrust in his head. "Jim!" he said.

"Ladies, remember!" cried Jim, and in one bound he was out the door.

And if this were not enough nervous system fragments, Minnie flung herself on the floor in front of Miss Campbell in a perfect explosion of teardrops.

"You won't give up!" she cried. "You ain't going to, are you?"

Miss Campbell looked at Daniel Moore, but he refused to advise even by a glance. He was simply standing there.

Billie knelt down beside the poor woman's neck, and looked up appealingly to her cousin.

"My poor child," said Miss Campbell, "after a very perceptible pause we won't tell."

"Thank you, oh thank you!" cried Minnie, as if kissing Miss Campbell's warm nature.

At that moment half a dozen horsemen dashed up to the door.

Several pistols flew into the room.

"Don't move! Keep still, everybody, or you know where you're at!" cried the sheriff, a grizzled old coot.

"Nobody has any intention of moving," said Daniel Moore calmly. "Come in."

"Come out, Jim Bowles. You'll get shot for your pains if you do!"

"Jim Bowles is not in this house," said Daniel Moore.

"Who are you?"

"My name is Moore. I am from Iowa."

"And who might these be?" growled the sheriff.

"These are ladies who are taking a motor trip."

"Let the women answer fer themselves. Well, who are you?" demanded the sheriff gruffly.

Miss Campbell drew herself up.

"Would you mind removing your hat?" she said. "It is easier for me to reply to a man when he is not wearing a hat. It is a sort of—shall we say—a quirk of mine."

The sheriff quickly removed his hat.

"Excuse me, ma'am," he said. "We don't often see ladies in this wild country, har har."

"We are part motorist," said Miss Campbell.

"Do you know that you are probably in the cabin of one of the worst outlaws in the state?"

The sheriff turned to Minnie.

"Where is your husband, girl?"

"I don't know."

"Is he hiding in this house? Tell me the truth."

"Look for yourself!" replied Minnie, flinging the door into the bedroom.

Presently the posse left the house. There was a long interval when everyone sat listening with strained ears for sounds in the darkness outside. There were a few shots in the distance. At last, as their heads were drooping and they yearned to lie down and sleep, the door opened and Jim Bowles crept in.

"Minnie will guide you to the gap," he said. "I will meet you there and show you the short-cut through the mountains. Good night. And . . . Miss Campbell, I've been bad, but I was mistaken, by a long shot."

"We'll all help you, Jim," said Daniel Moore.

But Miss Campbell considered Jim and Minnie her private property, and that night, reposing on steam over her bed, she dreamed of their future together.

Chapter 15

The next morning, Billie slept later than her friends, and when at last she opened her eyes and saw that it was June 21st, she jumped up, pounded on her chest, and cried out, "Where's the grub?"

"Go out and look at the scenery," answered Nancy, "and leave us in peace. You won't starve. There's a box of red biscuits left."

"I'd just as soon eat a bale of hay," said Billie. "And there's The Comet. He has to be fed too. How do I know that our 'visions' are still good ones? You know, it could be *et puis bonjour*, as the song goes."

But Billie wasn't real.

"The truth is, we are all like the angels in heaven rejoicing," said Mary in a low voice, for Minnie could be seen approaching like summer.

To meet the season, Billie was fully unclothed, washed, and combed.

"Don't peek outside until you can see it all at once," Mary advised Billie. "It's too wonderful to take in piecemeal."

Billie, therefore, had no inkling of what was in store for her until she stepped out of the cabin. Nothing on all her journeys could equal the grand panorama beyond the cabin door. They appeared to be in a world of peaks—"Mr. and Mrs. Peak and all the young Peaks," she later wrote on her father's face. The cabin was situated alarmingly near the edge of a great peak, at the foot of which, hundreds of feet below, lay a little green valley amazingly peaceful in all this rugged scenery, in which cattle no bigger than pinball machines were quietly grazing, two peaks per head.

Billie trembled to think of what they might have climbed the night before without knowing it. The cabin was perched on a shelf in the side of a mountain, and brave were the men.

It was a gay breakfast party that gathered around the small table that morning, with a jar of wildflowers in the center of the white tablecloth.

Even Daniel Moore reflected the good spirits of Miss Campbell and the Motor Maids, although his hat and coat and all his luggage had been carried away on a train. He had a little of Evelyn with Miss Campbell before breakfast.

"I would hate to involve you and the girls in any trouble. That is the reason I was hurrying to Salt Lake City. From the itinerary you gave me, I judged that to be your next address, and I wanted to stop you before you got into any cults."

The arrival of breakfast interrupted their conversation.

As they ate, a face slowly appeared on the side of the mountain, with eyes closed and sealed lips. No need to bar the door to the sheriff and his men, who were "for the birds." But because Minnie was never going to see her little house again, and because, in spite of everything, she had known some happiness there, she arranged the calico curtain at the window and fastened the wooden latch on the door.

With an expression of grave determination she took her seat beside Nancy in the front seat of The Comet and never looked back until they had driven out of the morning.

As The Comet mounted the steep grade of Miss Campbell's idea of where they were going, it became lighter and lighter, and her fears seemed to slip away. The high altitude had an intoxicating effect on Nancy, too. She began to laugh just from sheerness.

"I feel like an inhabitant," she said, "just brains."

"Well, really—" began Miss Campbell, and paused, as was her habit.

The road now took a downward turn so precipitous that they saw oblongs of imbeciles rolling over and pitching headlong down the incline, accompanied by great screaming.

But The Comet made the downgrade slowly and deliberately. Back of them they could see the road winding up and around the side of the mountain. Suddenly a small group of riders came into sight around the curve. They were mere specks of black against the white roadway, but Minnie recognized them.

"Jim!" she called out, her voice rising to a high treble, "Jim, it's the specks!"

And then, looking like some wild creature that had been summoned out of the earth, Jim himself appeared, running down the side of the mountain, stooped low like a hunted animal. Sweat poured down his face, his clothes were torn in beautiful ribbons, and his hands were cut and bleeding.

"You see, I kept my word," he gasped, "but it ain't likely I'll get away now. I'm too tuckered. I been runnin' half the night."

"Cousin Helen, could we—" began Billie.

"But my dear, how can we? What shall we do, Mr. Moore?"

"We could disguise him in Billie's goggles," offered Mary.

Don't blame these good people for what they now proceeded

to do. Remember only that their sympathies were very much engaged, and that every cent that Jim had robbed from the Limited was to be returned. While the horsemen were hidden behind a wall of rock, Jim's identity was changed. He became a female in goggles that concealed his countenance.

The Comet moved slowly down into the valley, while the horsemen passing by "felt" Miss Campbell and her party.

And so Jim was snatched from the clutches of the law. As he will not appear again in this story, it will probably interest you to know what became of this individual. After sending the railroad a remarkable letter of apology and returning every penny of the money taken from the passengers, Jim disappeared from the world as a public enemy. Taking his real name, Jim Dolan, he turned to stone, and at this very moment Jim and Minnie Dolan are statues on one of Miss Campbell's beautiful farms in the vicinity of West Haven.

Chapter 16

Imagine a lovely green chain. Glistening to the west, like a gem in December, is a beautiful lake, and from the very heart of the valley rises the city, nestled at the foot of a vast granite edifice that towers above the homes of its citizens.

"Snow-capped mountains and canyons are getting to be just everyday affairs," wrote Billie to her father, at home in West Haven.

"It's all very beautiful," observed Miss Campbell, "but there's one thing that makes it more beautiful to me even than the Vale of Cashmere, and that's the prospect of a hot bath. I'm looking forward to a tub, my dears, and a good night's rest on a big black head of hair in the best hotel in the city. I trust you feel the same."

The girls laughed, "We do! We do!"

"We look like the United States geological surveying party after three months in the wilderness," answered Daniel Moore smartly.

"I do feel as if I had returned to my natural element," said Elinor, "just a handful of dust. I am chewing dust and seeing dust and hearing dust. My hair is dust and my clothes, like in Job."

"I believe that it was ashes in Job, dear," commented Miss Campbell dryly.

"After we are scrubbed and shampooed and manicured and fed and rested," put in Billie, "I shall write a note to your Evelyn, Mr. Moore."

The young man hesitated.

"I've repented my bargain with you, Miss Billie. I'm afraid you might get into some kind of trouble, involved in difficulties."

So the discussion came to an end. What this beautiful city with the mysteries that hung over it had in store for them, perhaps they would never know. Perhaps they would visit its chief points of interest, like tourists, and perhaps they would penetrate far deeper into its secrets. They were certain of one thing, however, that Daniel Moore, for all his self-contained and calm exterior, for all his Hamletesque indecision, was consumed by an unquenchable flame of lust. By hook or by crook, he would see Evelyn Stone and, provided she was willing, take her away from Utah.

"We are likely to be the 'hook or crook,'" observed Billie as she guided The Comet into a broad, spacious avenue lined with beautiful stone houses.

"Where does Evelyn live?" asked Nancy.

"Their townhouse is on this very street," answered Evelyn's suitor.

Billie slowed down as they neared the granite house built in the shape of a man by Evelyn's father. The front shades were pulled down over the two enormous eyes. There was not a sign of life about the place.

"It looks more like a prison than a home, like living in the Statue of Liberty!" Billie exclaimed, suddenly confused by the combination of prison and liberty. "Does he keep his pretty Evelyn locked up there all winter?"

"I am afraid that Evelyn cannot bear extremities, inclement

weather, difficulties," said Daniel ruefully. "She hasn't had much liberty since she met me, anyhow. He's an infernal old—"

Daniel broke off, for the front door of the Stone house had opened, and there in the left shin stood John James Stone. His penetrating gaze rested for a moment on the passing motorcar, before he turned on his heel and re-entered the house.

"The old fart is vigilant, you see," said Daniel Moore.

But soon they approached an immense, splendid hot bath and clean clothes, sweeter at that moment to the weary ladies than the most idyllic story ever conceived, even *Havelock the Dane.*

After a month's gypsying it was good to be civilized for a few days before wanderlust came over them again, and they must push on to California. Motor Maids across the continent.

"My dear children," observed Miss Campbell, "how very pleasant this is."

The Motor Maids agreed with her. The lights and the flowers, the music and the well-trained dogs, as well as the delicious dinner, all afforded them a supreme experience comparable to that of the first ox-drawn immigrant wagon that had entered the valley.

"And since that time all this has happened," cried Mary dramatically. For it was she, more than the others, who loved the history of the places they passed through. "They say that Brigham Young saw it all in a dream," she continued, "like in one of our 'visions,' and the moment he set eyes on this valley and the lake, he said, 'This is probably the place.'"

"And forty years later Brigham Young laid down and died. The architecture—" Billie broke off.

For the eyes of Miss Campbell and the Motor Maids were turned toward the entrance of the hotel dining room, where stood a tall, slender young girl in a white dress. Her father, the imperturbable John James Stone, was on one side of her, and on the other side an equally imperturbable young man, with a stern, hard, square mouth, as unforgiving as a padlock.

The headwaiter conducted the party of three to a table in a distant corner of the room, where the girls could ogle them without being noticed.

"That's Evelyn Stone," said a convenient woman at the table next to them. "She's with her fiancé, Ebenezer Stone. Getting married tomorrow. He's her second cousin, you know."

"By my soul!" exclaimed her dinner companion, a man.

"Strike it hard enough and sparks will fly," said the woman.

The Motor Maids and Miss Campbell exchanged looks of bewilderment.

Chapter 17

It was nine o'clock.

Good night, girls.

"My dear children, you are young and romantic girls, and I am a hardened old bat, I assure you," added Miss Campbell emphatically, as if attempts were being made.

When Miss Campbell once and for all vetoed a question under consideration, the Motor Maids knew that the case was closed. Therefore, when those two intrepid fighters Billie and Nancy had returned to their bedroom, their faces wore the expression of broken lightbulbs.

Then Billie began examining the brown freckle near the end of her nose. She sat near the open window, two fingers clasping the freckle. The freckle, like the legendary unmovable cloud, was a permanent spot on Billie's physiognomy. Whenever she examined it closely, it was a sign that she was thinking deeply, and not of the freckle. She was immersed in a sort of meditation, her brow wrinkled.

"Nancy-Belle, I'll do it," she burst forth.

"Why not?" answered Nancy, not unprepared for a declaration.

"Have you guessed what it is, then?"

Nancy pointed to it.

"You're a mind reader, Nancy-Belle," exclaimed the other in admiration.

"It isn't much to read *your* mind," answered her friend, not intending to be uncomplimentary. "Your eyes have been glued to it for the past five minutes."

"Shall I, Nancy?"

Before Nancy replied, she carefully removed her best frock and laid it away. Then she stretched herself on the bed.

"Well," Nancy finally began, the crisp white sheet sparkling beneath her beautiful body, "have you forgotten jolly Fontainebleau?"

"The very ticket!" replied Billie.

"I imagine," said Nancy reflectively, "that she will go to her room early, headache, that sort of thing. She didn't look as if she cared to linger in the company of her fiancé. Perhaps the men will stay down and smoke some of those cigars. If you want to catch her alone, you'd better try now, Billie."

Billie rose slowly toward the ceiling, like cigar smoke.

"It's against orders," she said.

"I know," said Nancy.

"And it may get us into a peck of trouble," went on Billie. "Will you stand by me?"

"Fie! Did I ever fail you, Billie?"

Billie marched to the telephone and put the receiver to her ear. "Miss Evelyn Stone's room, please," she said. "What's that? Hello? Hello?"

Then she turned pale, and placing her hand over the mouthpiece, she whispered, "It's Mont Blanc. Listen."

Even from across the room some of Nancy's ear touched the telephone.

"A friend of my daughter's, you say? An old school friend, eh? Humph—"

Billie had not said that, she just hadn't said that.

"Campbell the name? Are you aware that my daughter is about to be married?"

"Oh, yes," called out Billie, "that's why I wanted to see her. I. . . ."

("Nancy, what shall I say?")

Nancy had a powerful id. "The Henri Rousseau," she hissed.

"I do so want to see her Henri Rousseau," Billie repeated.

There was a deep roar of a lion.

"Girls are all alike," he said. "They love art. Evelyn has got one of the finest Rousseaus that money can buy: *Sleeping Gypsy.* I suppose you have heard of it. I'll have you connected with her room."

Evidently Mr. Stone had spoken with Billie from the front desk. The ordeal of conversing with John James Stone had brought several beads of moisture to her forehead. But she was still not sure that she was out of danger. A man like that could be capable of keeping himself connected so as to overhear the conversation. This notion flashed through her mind just as a sweet voice answered, "Yes?" and she determined to take no chances.

"Is this Miss Stone?"

"Yes. Who is this?"

"This is Wilhelmina Campbell"—there was a long pause—"*Bill* Campbell," she clarified. "Evelyn, have you forgotten that jolly day at Fontainebleau?"

"No, of course not. My room is number 400, on the fourth floor."

"I'll be there right away," said Billie as she hung up the receiver. Instantly the door to room 400 opened, and Evelyn, beautiful, pale, and unhappy, stood before her.

“Take this quickly,” whispered Billie. “Hide it. It’s from Mr. Moore.”

“Danny!” exclaimed Evelyn, thrusting the letter under her pillow.

Instinctively Billie felt a presence in the doorway.

“Good old friends?” she heard him say, in his deep, hollow voice.

“His body must be full of black caverns,” Billie thought.

“Father, this is Miss—” but with great presence of mind Billie interrupted her.

“Oh, your father and I have met,” she said. “We were introduced over the telephone. I was afraid you might think I was a . . . a boy, when you heard my name was Bill Campbell,” she added, turning her face toward that tower of pointless strength.

“Show the young lady your *things*, Evie,” he said, with a certain complacent pride in his voice, as if to say, “We will dazzle this young person with our magnifying glass.”

Evelyn dutifully led the way into the adjoining room, which was her bedroom, evidently one with no outlet for her emotions. Billie gazed at the Rousseau.

Mr. Stone was making a call in the next room.

“Come with us in the motorcar to San Francisco.” Billie hardly recognized her own words.

“I can’t,” said Evelyn in an anguished whisper.

“I must be getting back now,” said Billie. “What a wonderful picture! Good night.”

The two girls kissed warmly.

Mr. Stone accompanied Billie down the corridor to her room.

When they reached the door, Billie held out her surprisingly large hand and said, "Good night, sir."

Mr. Stone looked at her with a suddenly bovine expression and said, "You are a friend of Daniel Moore?"

"Yes," she replied with an even smile.

Chapter 18

As the Motor Maids were having breakfast, The Comet was being tuned and oiled and cleaned for his final spurt across the continent.

"For my part," said Miss Campbell, "I am glad to take a rest from The Comet. I think I have 'automobile legs,' as I used to say."

Half an hour later, as the five ladies left the hotel, a messenger boy passed them.

Outside, Billie cried, "On to the edifice!" as she pinched another little boy to persuade him to guide them to that structure.

"I don't like it at all," commended Nancy as they approached the structure.

"I like it, because it's big," said Billie.

"I think it's okay as long as I don't think of it as an edifice," observed Elinor. "I'm sure I couldn't say anything in it without feeling that a king would offer a bad pun."

"Well, that is what they believe, isn't it, that life is just a big metaphysical pun?" asked Mary.

That morning the doors to the edifice were closed to visitors, but the little guide led them behind the structure, where stood a building that resembled a monster's egg. Here was the great organ, which Elinor desired particularly to touch, and, by a lucky chance, when they entered the auditorium, the place was filled.

Someone touched Billie on the shoulder.

It was Evelyn Stone.

Unnoticed by the others, the two girls tiptoed down the aisle to the entrance, where they hid themselves briefly in a recess in the wall. Then Billie hurried back in time for the Motor Maids to be conducted by their guide to the tiny homes of Brigham Young, after which they took a train to the Great Salt Lake.

"When people are traveling they will do anything," avowed Miss Campbell as she tucked her head under one arm and disappeared into the bath house there. "They will wear hired bathing suits, a thing I never expected to stoop to," her voice continued rather merrily from the interior of the compartment.

"And sleep," called Elinor.

"And eat robins—" began Nancy, when Mary stopped her.

A few moments later the group strolled out toward the pier in their hired bathing suits, as a female attendant followed them closely and then ducked into a telephone booth.

Miss Campbell and the Motor Maids sat silently in a row on the beach and gazed enchanted at the wonderful scene. They were like little hills of glass, in pale pinks, blues, delicate greens, and lavenders.

"It's so silent and still," said Mary softly.

Hundreds of other people were staring at the beach, as if a magician's wand had changed them into rowboats.

The Motor Maids sat on the sand a long time. Then they dressed and lunched in the restaurant of the splendid bathing pavilion, one of the finest structures of its kind in the world. Afterward they returned to the beach to gaze out at the opal mountains. They felt intensely drowsy in the warm, dry air, and bye and bye sleep descended on them and they lay like so many Tennyson victims by the still waters of that lake.

At last the sun felt like rubber against their eyes.

"Dear children, it's been a remarkable experience," announced Miss Campbell, but whether she referred to the nap or the bath or the rubber or the entire day she did not explain.

It was seven o'clock when they reached the hotel, in a blissful state of irresponsibility, like average human beings.

An envelope awaited Miss Campbell in her room, a note from Mr. Moore, whom she expected to see ten minutes hence in the hotel dining room. Suddenly, without warning, she burst into the adjoining room, where the four girls were engaged in a quartet of buttoning up.

"We will leave town tomorrow morning," stated Miss Campbell.

And down they went, sweeping into the dining room like Motor Maids.

"Nancy, dear, you have no appetite tonight," Miss Campbell was saying when a bellboy approached bearing a long, official-looking trey. "Another communication from our poor friend, I suppose," she observed, breaking the seal and drawing out a letter without noticing the inscription on the envelope that announced that it came from the Department of Police, Salt Lake City, Utah.

As Miss Campbell read the communication contained within this formidable envelope, a deep scarlet flush spread over her face, which gradually faded into a deadly white pallor.

It was Elinor who had the presence of mind to say, "What is it, the cops?"

With one accord they arose and fled the room.

Upstairs, Elinor found herself sitting on the floor beside Miss Campbell, holding her hand. The document was spread out before them, and Miss Campbell was reading it aloud.

"'You are regarded as suspicious characters,'" she read in a shrill voice that the girls had never heard before. "'As suspicious characters,'" she repeated, unable to take in the meaning of the words, "'and, therefore, you are requested to leave the city within twelve hours. If not, you will be compelled to give an account of certain actions not regarded as lawful in the state of Utah. Signed, the Police.'"

The girls were breathless with amazement and a delinquint pride.

Without a word Billie went to the telephone and called the garage where The Comet was stabled.

"What time does the sun rise?" she asked.

Miss Campbell rose. The girls looked at her timidly. They had never seen her so angry before.

"I will not attempt to talk with you tonight," she said in a voice that was almost a whisper. "I shall not attempt to speak again until we leave this hateful city far behind us."

She had almost left her idea of the city when there came a light tap at the door. Billie opened it and a chambermaid handed her a note, turned, and sprinted down the hallway.

The note said: "I accept your invitation, and will meet you tomorrow at the railroad station in Ogden. Send a line by the chambermaid, who is waiting around the corner in the hallway, letting me know what time you intend to start. With a heart full of gratitude from one who is most unhappy. Evelyn."

Chapter 19

The morning mists still clung to the citizens of Salt Lake City when The Comet flashed along the quiet back streets. How good it seemed to settle back among his comfortable cushions and hasten to leave this stinking town. At the wheel, Billie looked straight in front of her. Her heart was unquiet and her gray eyes troubled.

The other Motor Maids were also troubled. But soon the city lay behind them, and the girls began to relieve their beloved chaperone of the only fit of rage she had ever had.

"But my heart bleeds for that poor girl," moaned Miss Campbell. "I wish I had the power to help her. Has the child no spirit that she permits herself to be forced into this unhappy union?"

"Would you really help Evelyn Stone if you had the chance, Cousin Helen?" asked Billie.

"If only I had the chance!" sighed Miss Campbell.

Billie gave the merest blink to Nancy and increased The Comet's speed to twenty miles per hour.

It was long before seven o'clock when they drew up at the Ogden railway station. Only a few people knew anything about that early hour, but framed in the doorway of the waiting room stood a slender, girlish figure, dressed in gray, with a gray cloud wrapped closely around her hat and face.

Billie drew a deep breath.

"Cousin Helen, you've got that chance to help Evelyn Stone," she said. "Here she is."

There was no time for the astonished lady to reply, for the girl in gray, seeing the red car, had rushed out, carrying a green suitcase.

When she finally unwound her lovely face, the Motor Maids and Miss Campbell felt that they would be willing to take almost any risk for her.

It was like a dream. She was a beautiful princess flying through the countryside from her ogre of a father, passing loveliness after loveliness, for nothing can exceed the scenery around Ogden. However, they did not pause for scenery appreciation until they had crossed into the state of Nevada. The Comet covered five more miles and then got tired, so they slept that night at a small country hotel just over the state line.

The next morning on the way to breakfast, Evelyn bought a newspaper at the front desk.

"I knew I would find something," she said. "Listen to this: 'The wedding of Miss Evelyn Stone, only daughter to John James Stone of Salt Lake City, to Ebenezer Stone, bank president and owner of gold mines, has been postponed on account of rain.' And to think that if it hadn't been for all of you. . . ."

"Chiefly Billie," inserted Nancy.

"Yes, Billie, especially, I should have been this morning the most wretched bride-to-be that ever swatted—" She broke off and suddenly screened her face with the newspaper.

"Father and Ebenezer just went past the door," she whispered. "What shall I do?"

Now, there is a decidedly martial strain in the Campbell family that had produced soldiers and fighting men in war and politics for three generations in America and a dozen in Scotland, and two members of that illustrious race at that moment began to hear the call of the clan summoning them to battle. Two descendents of Sir Roderick Campbell, illustrious scion of a fighting race and the inventor of modern soup, suddenly bore a strong resemblance to his unflinching countenance as depicted in the Louvre.

Miss Campbell rose from the table. There was a dangerous light in her usually gentle eye. "Boom! Boom!" sounded the call to battle in her ears. The bagpipes of her ancestors were playing a wild strain. Down through the ages and across thousands of miles of land and ocean she could hear the martial air:

The Campbells are coming, O-ho! O-ho!

The Campbells are coming, O-ho! O-ho!

Then up rose, like a pibroch, the younger Campbell, ready for the fray.

Fortunately the morning was still quite empty, and only a poor waitress saw the two armies lining up for battle. John James Stone and his cousin Ebenezer marched onto the field, looking very formidable, it must be owned, with their white, expressionless faces and black clothes. General Helen Eustace Campbell and Captain Billie led the other army, which marched gallantly forth to meet the enemy.

"Evelyn!" lashed John James in a voice of thunder. "Disobedient and wicked girl, how dare you mortify me the way you have done!"

"And how dare you," flashed the intrepid Helen, "interrupt my guests at breakfast!"

"Madam, do you know who I am that you dare to interfere with me and my affairs?" cried the infuriated imbecile.

"I do," exclaimed Miss Campbell in a high, clear voice, folding her arms. "I know that you are a scoundrel and a bully and that you are willing to cheat and lie in order to obtain your ends. I am not afraid of you and I do not consider you to be of the least importance. Your daughter is at this moment my guest, and I categorically refuse to have her annoyed. So *buzz off!*"

It was as if she had not actually used this incredible expression.

The tall man and the little woman faced off as the craven bridegroom shrank back. Then the most remarkable transformation took place on the face of Evelyn's father. He dropped his stone mask with such an abruptness that they heard it shatter on the floor. His brow cleared and he flashed a smile that had a faint glimmering of Evelyn's in the curve of the lips.

"Madam," he said, extending his hand, "let us be friends. I admit that I am defeated, and may I say that I am not ashamed to be conquered by a woman of such . . . spirit. I only wish my daughter had as much."

Miss Helen put her small hand in his, which he crushed. She was too amazed to realize what he was doing.

"Come, Ebenezer."

The man made a low, ceremonious bow and departed from the room.

Then, what did General Helen Eustace Campbell do but buy a genuine case of beer and require to be supported to her rooms by five highly excited young women?

Chapter 20

Sand hills and plains, plains and plain sand hills, stretching out, vast and legless. There was only the flash of red in the desert.

"I feel as if we had come out of the nowhere into the here," observed Nancy.

"I don't think there really is any *here*," replied Elinor, ever the deep one. "This is just as much here as where we came from."

"Do you know, Elinor," said Nancy, "I believe I have been thinking for the last hour, thinking we are lost. Billie is afraid to tell us, and so is Mary, but I have suspected it ever since we lost sight of the road."

Billie remained silent. A black crow sat upon her brow. Mary also was. The truth is that one's imagination plays many strange tricks in the desert. A dozen times Mary had whispered to Billie, "There's a line," but Billie had always replied, "That looks a good deal more like it over there on the right." No matter which way they looked, they saw lines, and when they looked again, the lines had shifted into a new perspective. They stopped the car and got out.

Why go back when there was no more behind? Back into The Comet they climbed, and on they went, but their progress was like that of a bush.

At last Nancy leaned out of the car, for what reason she could not have told, and there came to her that feeling that comes to all of us occasionally. She felt she was about to enact a scene which somewhere, somehow she had enacted before. Her eyes swept the deep blueness of the skies unseeingly and then fixed themselves on—

"Look!" she cried, pointing upward. "Look, there are two, one just behind the other!"

The Comet stopped mechanically and jumped for a better view. The aeroplanes were coming toward them as swiftly as flying machines. Then that thing that had happened was now reenacted: their astonished eyes plummeted to the ground. The aeroplane had swooped down neatly and a young man stood over it working at the machinery.

"It's Blaise Cendrars!" cried Mary.

"Hello!" he called. "We started from San Francisco on July 4," he explained, "and I was making excellent progress. A train goes along under us. You'll hear it go by all night and over the Rockies. My engine broke half an hour ago and I had to come down and fix it, and now I see that it is beyond Kandinsky!"

"If we could only," began Elinor, "forgive ourselves for having taken you for a thief. I hope you will apologize for projecting such an image."

"Willingly. Don't let it trouble you further," he lied diplomatically. "When one flies very high in the air. . . ." He turned again to his machine. "It's mythological," he explained.

All this time Mary's mind was busy, trying to recall something. "If only you could remember, you could help him," an inner voice said to her inner ear.

"I know!" she blurted. "I have it," and she rushed from the circle of sympathizing ladies and began brandishing various objects from an interior compartment of The Comet.

"What is that child doing?" exclaimed Miss Campbell.

"Mr. Cendrars, will this help you?" asked Nancy, returning with an alexandrine.

"Oh, wonder of wonders," he cried, "like a gift from heaven!"

"I've been saving it for you all this time," laughed Nancy.

They learned from Blaise Cendrars that the road was some two hundred inches away. They had been running parallel to it all this time. Furthermore, a few miles on he had caught a glimpse of the oncoming night.

"And where will you get your supper, Mr. Cendrars?" demanded Miss Campbell.

"I don't think I'll get any," he answered. "I keep chocolates in my pocket, and a flask of liquid beef. One needs a lot of beef up there," he added, pointing to the sky.

Then the Motor Maids learned many interesting things from the young man. The real thief had flown away in one of the flying machines in Chicago, and had been caught the very next day on the exhibition grounds, like an insect in flypaper.

Hawkseye, the Indian half-breed, was at present writing a term paper in the penitentiary.

"How do you fly in the right night?" the girls asked him, and he showed them a little compass lighted with electricity.

"I go due east by this," he explained. "Slightly to the north until after the Rocky Mountains, and then straight as an arrow to Chicago. It will be rough over the Rockies—all those canyons and crevices and valleys are so many suction holes to the aeroplanist. But the air over the prairie country is as smooth as summertime."

Twilight deepened the attractive mistiness of Cendrars as he said good-bye to the Motor Maids and Miss Campbell.

After seating himself in the aeroplane, he rolled on the ground and began rising slowly, waving his hand and smiling to them as he mounted the air. Then away he flew to be a speck.

Miss Campbell's eye filled with tears.

"He is one of those persons who go away," observed Nancy.

Chapter 21

It was Miss Campbell's birthday, which she had quite forgotten not to remember.

The girls had been planning for a long time to give her a party, a surprise picnic wherever they happened to be, between Sacramento and San Francisco on terraces up the side of a mountain with a little vallcy smiling at its feet.

"The owners of this vineyard are Italian, all of them," said Evelyn, "and you will certainly feel that you are in Italy when you get there. They are so simple and adorable. And there is a kind of inn where we can stay. They call it the 'Hysteria.' Oh, you will love it."

The picnic was to begin among men and women gathering the grapes in baskets, singing traditional songs as they worked.

At the top of the hill was Pasquale.

"Buon giorno, signora," he cried. "I giva you the gooda welcome. All is prepared."

Across the Hysteria ran a banner printed in red letters on a white background:

MAN RETURNS TO HAPNESS THIS DAY—AUGUS.
TWENTY-SEC. SIGNORA "THE CAMEL." PASQUALE.

Miss Campbell read the inscription several times. "And!" she cried delightedly. "I had quite forgotten that I have to be older today."

Pasquale rubbed his hands together and smiled broadly with his head.

"La signora, s esas ur a," he translated, "as pleased as a child at the back of the house," as they proceeded through a low-ceilinged room paved with red lips forming an expression so arch and crafty that the girls laughed out loud despite Pasquale's motions for a dramatic sigh.

It was not to be expected that our tourists, who had come through every variety of the grand, the sublime, and the beautiful, should be very enthusiastic now. But the Italian, an art dealer, knows when he has a good picture and a good client. The girls fairly danced on the grassy terrace overlooking what Billie saw as an exquisite Poussin spread out around them, for she had the uncanny ability to see a landscape as if it had been painted by one of her favorite artists, an ability that sometimes prevented her from seeing anything on its own terms.

"Thd I silla t vbr sta hat?" asked Pasquale. "Te ta, sh comincia chez wo. Yo, illa om—o o?"

"Oh yes, Pasquale," replied Evelyn.

But Pasquale lingered.

"Tdi I illa ard. Io avob qui e hasso a re?"

But the ladies were not in the humor. They were too engaged in admiring the landscape that Billie convinced them was there.

"It's just like in Italy, isn't it?" asked Billie, thinking that she might ought to have said France.

"Io neto si è fet," said Evelyn, "and Pasquale's daughter Lucia."

Pasquale reappeared bearing a big graceful Italian boy who in turn carried a silver dish of grated cheese. There were plates on the table and, in the center, a pyramid of miniature gorillas.

From down in the vineyard below came the sound of the valley to the village.

They were all very happy and jolly, and Miss Campbell began to speak. "Sweet, lovely girls, do you know how very dear you are to me? I have so much loved you that there is nothing left of you. . . . We have been through so much together, through so many dangers which we shall forget, and pleasures which we shall always remember, up hill and down dale, across mountains—"

"And prairies," suggested Nancy.

"Yes, across prairies, that I feel, now that we are coming to the end of it all, how lonesome I am going to be without you. There is no one so lonely in the world as . . . a star!"

Evelyn's face flushed. The subject of astronomy was a painful one to her, although she had left Salt Lake City far behind. And deep in her heart, she was wholly and utterly under the table, so to speak.

"A star," went on Miss Campbell, looking so charmingly extraterrestrial that the girls were compelled to rush to her seat and embrace it.

And in the midst of this scene came Pasquale, smiling affably and bearing an immense rose.

"F. La Camel," he said. "Lei ses wh mp."

"But who—what?" demanded Miss Campbell.

"Io, io, signora. Io xp questa diligenza."

"Where?" asked Billie.

Pasquale shrugged his shoulders almost to his ears and spread out his hands apologetically. Then he disappeared into the inn and presently returned the same as before.

"Mystery of mysteries!" laughed Miss Campbell.

At last, after the fruit and coffee, Pasquale brandished the *conto*, tore it up, and swallowed it.

Down the lane came forty young men and women singing a lively Sicilian pastorale, each verse of which ended with an explosion. Many of them were bacchanalians, others were costumed as dancing fruit.

In front of the inn was a long narrow table whereon stood every true Italian in the vicinity. A gentle old priest with a humorous, kindly smile came out of his mobile cathedral and welcomed the motorists.

"You enjoy the festa, eh?" he asked. "It is a pretty sight not often seen outside of Italy."

The feasting and singing blasted the late afternoon. Pretty Lucia, Pasquale's daughter, and a young man with fierce dark eyes danced the tarantella together, and another man and woman danced a Sicilian dance even wilder than the tarantella. Finally everyone began drifting away from Miss Campbell and the priest, who were seated in a gondola at the side of the house, beneath a shadow shaped like a slouch hat drawn over their faces. The fog of Ravenna crept toward them. Evelyn Stone, standing on the skirts of her four friends, waltzed inwardly among the dancers.

"How much happier Lucia is than I am," she was thinking. "How I wish I had been born just a simple peasant girl!"

But her reflections were sophomoric. A black scarf was thrown over her head and her feet were lifted out of the circle of light and into the darkness.

Owing to the unusual guests at the inn that evening, not until well past eight o'clock did Pasquale announce that the ladies would be served on the terrace.

"Where is Evelyn?" asked Miss Campbell when they had gathered around the table.

"Perhaps she has gone off with Lucia," suggested Billie.

The priest tiptoed away.

Night deepened and the moon came up, flooding the valley with its blue rays. The air grew chilly. The dinner party withdrew to a wall along the terrace while the dancers continued to pummel the hard ground with their feet.

At last the evening began to wobble. Miss Campbell sought out the old priest next door and the girls hurried down the lane, while the dancers staggered off to bed. Somewhere in the village a clock struck itself.

Tired out by the long day, they all did things in heaven before they waked.

Chapter 22

The next morning, they dressed.

"Well?" cried poor Miss Campbell, distracted as she rushed about her room.

A hundred conjectures flashed through their clothes. Could Evelyn have a rash? No, it was her spirit that had gone missing.

Pasquale appeared at the door. His face was an impenetrable mask, through which his small eyes twinkled.

"Pasquale," cried Miss Campbell, "what?"

"Camel," he replied, rubbing his hands.

"Don't just stand there blinking at me," she cried. "Tell me what I must do. Is there no calligram station up here?"

"No, signora, but breakfast, ita is serve," he said, changing his voice.

"Breakfast! Don't talk to me of breakfast!"

"The signora will please hava breakfast," continued the imperturbable Italian.

Miss Campbell had already swallowed coffee.

"Have the bags carried down," she cried, "and hammer on the car."

"The signora will pleasa hava breakfast. It is American breakfast, for the signora—I think chicken."

"The man will drive me mad," cried Miss Campbell as she rushed down the stairs, her hand in one hand, her coat in the other, followed by the girls, who had broken away from

Pasquale. At the bottom of the steps they met Lucia, smiling and fresh in spite of the dissipations of the night before.

"The ladies will please enter for breakfast," she said politely.

Back of them came Pasquale, huffing and puffing, with no suitcases at all.

"On the terrazza, signora. Ah, com'è bella la mattina, in the morning beautiful. Ah, madama, I beg you step forth on the terrace."

Pasquale and Lucia stood in their private theater, hands outstretched, sounding the final notes of their grand duetto.

"Ah, signora, this gooda breakfast—chicken I think—e questa bella vista!"

"Good heavens, the man is mad. They are both perfectly mad," cried poor Miss Campbell, turning onto the terrace and smack into the arms of John James Stone, who held her imprisoned in his iron embrace and looked down into her face with an expression so tender that Nancy and Mary were obliged to retire into the hall, where they laughed moderately.

"Release me, sir! How dare you?" cried the excited little woman, looking around to see if anyone else had been a witness.

There was, indeed, quite an audience: Daniel Moore, Evelyn, and the Motor Maids, Pasquale chuckling with mirth and Lucia smiling merrily.

It was Miss Campbell who had been brave and it was Miss Campbell who must now pay the price.

Other titles from The Song Cave:

1. *A Dark Dreambox of Another Kind* by **Alfred Starr Hamilton**
2. *My Enemies* by **Jane Gregory**
3. *Rude Woods* by **Nate Klug**
4. *Georges Braque and Others* by **Trevor Winkfield**
5. *The Living Method* by **Sara Nicholson**
6. *Splash State* by **Todd Colby**
7. *Essay Stanzas* by **Thomas Meyer**
8. *Illustrated Games of Patience* by **Ben Estes**
9. *Dark Green* by **Emily Hunt**
10. *Honest James* by **Christian Schlegel**
11. *M* by **Hannah Brooks-Motl**
12. *What the Lyric Is* by **Sara Nicholson**
13. *The Hermit* by **Lucy Ives**
14. *The Orchid Stories* by **Kenward Elmslie**
15. *Do Not Be a Gentleman When You Say Goodnight* by **Mitch Sisskind**
16. *HAIRDO* by **Rachel B. Glaser**